THE SECRET

KEN McCLURE is an award-winning medical scientist as well as a internationally acclaimed author. He was born and brought up in Edinburgh, Scotland, where he studied medical sciences and cultivated a career that has seen him become a prize-winning researcher in his field. Using this background to base his thrillers in the world of science and medicine, he is currently the author of twenty-four novels and his work is available across the globe in over twenty languages. He has visited and stayed in many countries in the course of his research but now lives in the county of East Lothian, just outside Edinburgh.

Visit his website at www.kenmcclure.com

REVIEWS

'His medical thrillers out-chill both Michael Crichton and Robin Cook.'

Daily Telegraph

'McClure writes the sort of medical thrillers which are just too close to plausibility for comfort.'

(Eye of the Raven) Birmingham Post

'Well wrought, plausible and unnerving.'

(Tangled Web) The Times

'A plausible scientific thriller . . . McClure is a rival for Michael Crichton.'

(The Gulf Conspiracy) Peterborough Evening Telegraph

'Contemporary and controversial, this is a white knuckle ride of a thriller.'

(Past Lives) Scottish Field

'Ken McClure looks set to join the A list at the top of the medical thriller field.'

Glasgow Herald

'McClure's intelligence and familiarity with microbiology enable him to make accurate predictions. Using his knowledge, he is deciding what could happen, then showing how it might happen . . . It is McClure's creative interpretation of the material that makes his books so interesting.'

The Guardian

THE SECRET

Ken McClure

Most of the places and institutions mentioned in this story are real, but all the persons described are entirely fictitious. Any resemblance between characters in the story and any real persons, living or dead, is purely coincidental.

This edition published in Great Britain in 2013 by Polygon, an imprint of Birlinn Ltd

West Newington House
10 Newington Road
Edinburgh
EH9 1QS

www.polygonbooks.co.uk

ISBN: 978 1 84697 261 4

British Library Cataloguing-in-Publication Data
A catalogue record for this book is available on request from the British Library

Typeset by Palimpsest Book Production Ltd, Falkirk, Stirlingshire
Printed and bound by Clays Ltd, St Ives plc

PROLOGUE

Laura McAllister opened the curtains in her daughter's bedroom and paused for a moment, feeling the morning sun on her face and thinking she should count her blessings. Life was good. She had a loving husband in a well-paid government job, a beautiful home here in Deansville, a small Maryland town situated halfway between Washington DC and Fort Detrick where Mark worked, and an adorable daughter Jade whose blonde curls currently spilled round her face on the pillow like a halo in the sunlight.

Laura sat down gently on the edge of the bed and ran her fingertips lightly across Jade's forehead. 'Good morning, birthday girl,' she whispered. 'Who is four years old today?'

It took a few moments for the question to make its way through the land of nod and bring Jade to consciousness; then she opened her eyes and broke into a big smile. 'I am,' she said excitedly.

'Happy birthday, darling.'

Hugs and kisses later, Jade began looking past her mother and Laura moved out of the way so she could see the colourful pile of presents waiting for her.

'Yippee.'

Laura squatted on the floor beside Jade to help with the unwrapping and to identify the source of each present. She waited until they'd all been opened and the succession of oohs and aahs had abated before saying, 'I think you'll find a rather special present through here.' She took Jade by the hand and led her into the living room where a large doll's house stood in the middle of the floor, the lights in its windows already switched on. 'Daddy built it for you, honey. What d'you think?'

'Wow,' said Jade. 'It's the best.' She explored the building from every angle, her eyes wide with delight. 'I wish Daddy was here, Mom.'

'So do I, honey, but he'll phone you later and he won't be away for long. Daddies with important jobs sometimes have to go away on business trips; he'll be back before you know it. Meanwhile, we've got a party to organise. All your friends are coming this afternoon and we have to make sure there's enough cake and ice cream for everyone.'

'Can we keep a piece of cake for Daddy?'

Laura felt a lump come to her throat. 'Of course we can, honey.'

The phone rang and Laura answered briefly before handing it to Jade. 'It's Grandma,' she said, and smiled broadly when she heard her mother and father singing Happy Birthday at the other end of the phone. It was shaping up to be a good day.

Several thousand miles away in Islamabad, Dr Mark McAllister was reflecting on his day. He was no great fan of long-distance travel but business-class flights from Washington to London and then on to Islamabad after only minimal delay had gone without a hitch. Having no personal knowledge of any country further east than France – which he had visited once on a student trip – he had been slightly worried about the conditions he might encounter in Pakistan, but his fears had been allayed by being met at the airport by someone from the embassy and driven in an air-contitioned car to the Islamabad Marriott Hotel, where he was now ensconced in a very comfortable room.

Mark was a molecular biologist, a lab scientist who'd worked for the US government since gaining his PhD some ten years before. The nature of his job meant limited contact with people and very little need to travel. This was especially true since he'd been seconded to the top secret facility at Fort Detrick, where his work was highly classified and even participation in international scientific conventions was not encouraged – even prohibited without careful scrutiny beforehand.

It had come as a surprise, therefore, when he'd been informed that his presence would be required at an intelligence meeting to be held in Islamabad – a top secret meeting called by the CIA, MI6 – the British secret service – and Pakistani intelligence. He had not even been allowed to tell his wife where he would be heading, only that he wouldn't be away for long. Happily, Laura, the daughter of a former colonel in the US army, understood how these things worked and accepted the situation without question, although knowing that he would miss out on his daughter's fourth birthday had been more painful. He had been briefed by a CIA officer beforehand about what he could and could not say at the meeting. 'We're allies in name only,' he was cautioned. 'Things can change quickly in Pakistan.'

Mark wasn't at all certain what this implied but took it to mean keep your mouth shut unless given the okay by the CIA. He still wasn't sure why he was there: he was a specialist in DNA manipulation not the war on terror. He spent his days cutting and pasting pieces of DNA molecules rather like journalists with words and phrases on their laptops. When seconded to Detrick he'd been asked to continue work on a project started by one of their scientists who had been called away on assignment to London. He'd been asked to design an activator and a deactivator for what had been termed an 'interesting molecule'. What it was exactly the powers-that-be had decided he didn't need to know, and he knew better than to ask.

Mark glanced at his watch: it was seven p.m. A ten-hour time differential meant that it would be nine in the morning in Maryland and the girls would be up and about. He called home using the hotel instruction card and was successful at the fourth attempt. He deduced immediately through hearing excitedly whispered questions that Laura had let Jade answer the phone.

'Daddy, Daddy, it's my birthday. I've got lots of presents and I'm going to have a party and all my friends are coming . . .'

Mark let the words wash over him, closing his eyes and picturing the scene at home until Jade asked if he wanted to speak to Mummy.

'Yes please, Jade. Daddy loves you very much, honey.'

'Come home soon, Daddy.'

Laura came on the line and asked about his journey, then told him all about the plans for the day. 'Wish I was there,' he said, feeling quite emotional. Little girls were good at doing that to their fathers.

'I hope the government doesn't make a habit of this,' Laura joked.

'They won't,' replied Mark. 'I'm pretty sure this is a one-off. No one has said anything about doing any lab work here so I'm figuring that I'm just meant to be some kind of consultant to bring the other guys up to speed. After that, I should be homeward bound.'

'No need to pin a yellow ribbon on the apple tree in the garden then?'

'None at all, honey.'

Mark felt much better for having spoken to Laura and Jade. He was now going to shower, change, have dinner over at the embassy and be given a personal briefing. After that, it had been suggested he have an early night. He would be picked up at six the following morning for 'quite a long drive'.

Mark was briefed by a CIA man named Brady. Brady had been present at dinner, where the conversation had largely been embassy staff chatter about the conditions in Islamabad. Mark had been struck by how ordinary it had all sounded – they could have been working for an insurance company – but now he and Brady were alone in an upstairs room.

'I take it you've realised the molecule you've been working on is a virus?' Brady asked.

'Frankly, I'd expect to be fired if I hadn't,' joked Mark.

Brady nodded. 'You're here because your work on it has been going pretty well, by all accounts.'

'I think I've come up with what was requested of me, although there will have to be tests, of course.'

'Of course, and that's also why you're here. Your predecessor, now working in London, and his English associates have been having problems in designing what you've succeeded in doing. This will be a chance for you guys to get together and exchange information. I take it you have the details with you?'

Mark nodded, thinking it was a stupid question but limiting his reply to, 'I was told to bring them.'

'Encrypted?'

'Of course.'

'Good. Our friends in Pakistani intelligence know all about the virus and the initial field tests – they were instrumental in setting them up – but your side of things must remain confidential. Understood?'

Mark nodded uncertainly. 'The field tests?' he asked.

'We've been trying out the virus.'

'On people?' Mark asked, betraying disbelief.

'Yeah. It's OK; nobody died.'

'But that's . . .'

'Life, doctor,' Brady interrupted. 'Some of us have the privilege in life of doing what's decent, moral and honourable and some of us have to do what's necessary. Uncle Sam expects you to just do your job, OK?'

Mark agreed, feeling he was doing so on autopilot as he struggled to come to terms with what he was hearing but knowing that any protest he might make would probably result in his being asked what the hell he thought he was doing at Fort Detrick anyway: making toys for Christmas?

'Have you heard of the Khyber Pass, doctor?' Brady asked.

'Of course, in boyhood stories.'

'Tomorrow you'll be driving through it.'

Mark was the last to be picked up in the morning. He had been told it would be a low-key affair. This translated into two vehicles which looked military in origin with the ability to handle rugged terrain but lacking any markings. Brady introduced Mark to two others who would be travelling in their vehicle, a Pakistani intelligence officer named Faisal and a US marine driver named Mick. The other vehicle looked to contain four more marines, judging by their haircuts.

'Faisal hails from the Khyber Pakhtunkhwa,' said Brady.

Mark looked blank.

'It's the modern name for what used to be called the North West Frontier in your story books, doctor.'

'Now, a little less romantic, perhaps,' said Faisal, speaking perfect English with an accent that even sounded English to Mark's ear: he guessed at English schooling.

'A troubled place,' said Mark.

'Still is,' said Faisal. 'One of the English poets described it as having blood on every stone.'

'Let's hope for a quiet day,' said Brady. 'The others will be coming up from the Afghanistan side. We're meeting at a small village away from prying eyes.'

They fell to silence as the day wore on, Mark mesmerised by the mountains that towered above them on the ascent through the pass and thinking about the carnage they'd witnessed through the years.

'Not much longer now,' said Faisal to Mark before giving instructions to the driver. 'The vehicles can't manage the final stretch; it's too steep,' he explained. 'We'll be met.'

He made a call on what Mark noted was a satellite phone and ten minutes later they pulled off the road at the foot of a rough track that wound up into the mountains. A number of heavily bearded men in traditional dress were waiting there, sitting astride mopeds, automatic rifles slung across their backs.

'Not exactly Harley D's, are they,' murmured Brady, eyeing the bikes as they got out.

'I'm just relieved they're not donkeys,' Mark confessed.

Faisal and Brady agreed the order of travel for the pillion passengers. Faisal would be a passenger on the first bike with Mark riding pillion on the second, then Brady and finally two of the marines. Their driver Mick and the remaining marines would stay with the vehicles.

Mark, clutching his briefcase, mounted the second moped, looked for something to hold on to rather than the rider, and sent a nervous glance towards Brady, who smiled back. He took comfort from knowing that by travelling upwards they would remain in sunlight a little longer, avoiding the darkness which was already stalking the valleys below. The angry insect-like rasp of two-stroke engines rose to fever pitch and the party moved off through a blue fug of exhaust, the bike wheels scrabbling for grip on the loose stony path and sending a hail of pebbles over the edge of an increasingly precipitous drop. Mark closed his eyes and turned his face sideways to seek the shelter offered by his rider's back. He maintained this pose until the noise began to fade and the column drew to a stuttering halt at a spot where the track split into two.

Mark didn't know why they'd stopped but didn't care: he immediately took the chance to dismount and stretch his calf muscles, which had been threatening to cramp through being confined in the same position for such a long time. Surely they couldn't be lost? He was dusting himself down when Faisal walked over to him and said, 'This is your first time here, doctor. Come, you should see the view; it's something special.'

Brady nodded his agreement.

Mark could already see that the view was indeed spectacular, the dying rays of the sun turning the mountain tops red as far as the eye could see. He followed Faisal up on to a rocky promontory and gasped in admiration as all was revealed.

'Some say it's a reflection of the blood in the sky,' said Faisal of the crimson landscape.

Mark's imagination knew no bounds as he struggled to take in the rugged beauty of all that lay before him: he was on a distant planet in the outer reaches of the universe; he was a time traveller; he was a speck of dust in something that was infinite. Eventually, when reality made its pitch, he turned to thank his companion for the experience but was chilled to the bone by what he was confronted by. The demeanour of the pleasant, smiling man with the language and accent of an English public schoolboy had changed dramatically. The look in Faisal's eyes was one of pure hatred.

'What the . . .'

Faisal let out a yell and all hell was let loose as more than a dozen Kalashnikovs opened fire from the rocks above and around them. Brady and the others didn't stand a chance: they were mown down in a matter of seconds, leaving Faisal and Mark the only two of the party left alive. Two of the men from the rocks materialised beside Mark and pinned his arms behind his back as Faisal inspected the corpses on the ground, using his foot casually and apparently without emotion.

Mark felt trapped in a bad dream from which there was no escape: it was the running-in-mud scenario. He couldn't take his eyes off his erstwhile travel companions, their riddled bodies lying in pools of blood which were already drying into the dirt, and he seemed to have lost the power of speech. His throat had contracted to the point where he could only make gasping noises.

One of the bodies moved. Amazingly, Brady was still alive, though clearly mortally wounded. Mark saw he was looking up at him. 'Don't tell them, doctor . . . Don't fucking tell them . . .'

They were Brady's last words. A full stop was applied by Faisal putting a pistol shot through his head, causing his brains to splatter out over the stones and Mark to throw up.

Mark deduced that they were in some kind of cave complex when the blindfold was removed and he'd stopped blinking against the light. As a scientist, he immediately took on board that it was electric light, quickly correlating this with the distant but distinctive sound of a generator. Several computer monitors sat on a bench to his left. Two were manned by turbaned men; three others had screen-savers lazily doing their thing, tumbling cubes and fish going nowhere. Faisal stood there with an armed man on either side. 'You have something we want, doctor. I'd appreciate your cooperation. In fact . . . I must insist.'

'I don't know what you're talking about,' said Mark, glad he'd got the words out but afraid his insides were turning to water.

'Let's cut to the chase, shall we?' said Faisal, holding up a disk salvaged from the contents of Mark's briefcase, which were at his feet. 'This is encrypted; I need the key.'

Mark swallowed, his head swimming with all that had happened. *Cut to the chase?* he thought. *Cut to the fucking chase?* That was the sort of thing English actors said in some crummy olden-days drama on TV, not some fucking psycho in a cave in the middle of fucking nowhere. When would this nightmare end? His head lolled in silent appeal. 'I don't have it.'

'Shit,' said Faisal although not angrily, more as if it had been the response he'd been expecting and he was mildly irritated. He punched numbers into his satellite phone and then held it by his side until it beeped twice. He examined it and nodded in satisfaction before turning it round and holding it up in front of Mark's face. Laura and Jade filled the small screen. Their mouths were taped but their eyes spoke of the terror they felt. A knife blade hovered at Laura's throat. Jade wore a badge that said *I am 4*.

'Now, do we understand each other?'

The dam broke inside Mark and he unleashed every expletive he could think of at Faisal, who remained impassive throughout the outburst. When he finally ran out of energy and imagination, his curses degenerating into disjointed sobs and appeals, Faisal said simply, 'Give me the key.'

Mark, unable to take his eyes off Laura and Jade, nodded silently and was released from his bindings. He picked up his empty briefcase from the floor and said, 'I need a knife.'

Faisal nodded and one of the armed men handed Mark his knife, handle first, to the accompaniment of clicking gun mechanisms. Mark picked away at the stitching of an interior side panel of his briefcase and extracted a computer memory card. He handed it to Faisal, who passed it to one of the men sitting at the monitors. After a few moments, the man appeared satisfied and indicated as much to Faisal, who smiled. The intelligence agent took back the memory card and put it along with the disk he'd held up earlier in an envelope which Mark noted was marked *Vaccination schedules*. He handed the envelope to one of his men and told him where to take it, adding, 'When you get to the village, leave it at the clinic. Dr Khan will pick it up from there.' Then he turned to Mark, who was now suffering the agony of having betrayed his country on top of everything else.

Mark said, 'You've got what you wanted. Let my wife and daughter go.'

Faisal didn't bother with a reply. He nodded to the armed men flanking Mark and they gripped his arms to drag him outside, ignoring his questions and pleas before ending his suffering with a burst of gunfire that echoed off the surrounding rocks in a fading, repetitive requiem.

Back in Deansville, Laura's and Jade's lives also came to an end. Not being in the wilds of the Khyber, gunfire would have aroused suspicion in the small Maryland town, so a knife was used. What had started off as such a good day for the McAllister family had ended very badly indeed.

When Faisal received confirmation that the marines left to guard the vehicles down in the pass had been dealt with and that the vehicles themselves had been destroyed, he felt a warm glow of satisfaction. All he needed now was a message confirming that the information he'd obtained from the American had arrived safely at the pre-arranged collection point in the village for his mission to have been a complete success. He got it before sunrise.

When Faisal emerged from the cave complex to watch the sun come up, his conclusion that life was good was to be short-lived. He had underestimated the CIA man Brady who, unsure of whom or whom not to trust in Pakistani intelligence, had attached a tiny GPS transmitter to Faisal's clothing, thus ensuring that the CIA would know exactly where he was within a one-metre range of any spot on the planet. If for any reason Brady did not report back within an agreed period of time, a train of events would swing into operation. Brady was dead, but from beyond the grave he was responsible for a little black speck appearing in the morning sky as Faisal drew deeply on his first cigarette of the day. The speck was an unmanned drone that had locked on to Faisal's GPS signal.

The calm gaze with which Faisal watched the speck get bigger had barely time to change in response to the awful dawn of realisation before the drone unleashed its fiery equivalent of hell on earth and Faisal, together with his friends and accomplices, were all but vaporised in the firestorm that swept through the caves. The CIA wasn't to know that the information they wanted most to destroy wasn't actually there.

ONE

Dr Steven Dunbar parked the Porsche Boxster and got out to clamber over steep dunes to reach the beach, with the soft, dry sand and tufted grass begrudging him every step of the way. He needed to escape the travails of everyday life, to get his head straight, to think things through, and, as always, it was a beach he came to when milestones loomed large in his life. The location of the beach didn't really matter as long as it was deserted and afforded him views to the horizon with a big expanse of sky above, the bigger the better.

Today's beach was on the north shore of the Solway Firth in south-west Scotland – the part tourists rushed past on their way north to Loch Lomond in their haste to embrace the Walter Scott-manufactured myths of the Scottish highlands. Many of those who knew and loved the wild, romantic shores of the Solway were in no hurry to let the cat out of the bag and were aided in their desire for continuing anonymity by uneven sand banks, fast-flowing tides and quicksand lying in wait for the unwary.

Steven's milestones were the usual mix of sad and happy common to most folk – a time when a life-changing decision had to be made, the death of a parent, an impending marriage, the birth of a child and, in his case, the tragic loss of a wife through the ravages of a brain tumour. Today he'd learned of the death of a friend and needed to be alone. He'd been on leave up in Scotland visiting his daughter Jenny when the news had reached him. Sir John Macmillan, his boss and head of the Sci-Med Inspectorate in London, had phoned to tell him that Dr Simone Ricard of the

French-based but international charity *Médecins Sans Frontières* had been found dead. Macmillan had remembered that she'd been a friend of Steven's and thought it significant enough to interrupt his long weekend with the news. Currently he had no further information but would keep him informed if and when details came in.

Steven reached the water's edge and drew a line in the sand with his toe for no particular reason. It was clear enough today to see where the sky fell into the sea and this pleased him. It conferred a sense of order on the scene, unlike days when the heavens disappeared into the water in a miasma of grey nothingness. He thought about Simone and wondered, as he had so often in the past, how they had become friends in the first place. True, they were both doctors, but they could hardly have been more different in outlook.

Simone was French, the only child of professional parents – both university lecturers – who'd been born and brought up in Marseilles but had moved to Paris to complete her education and attend medical school. She had wanted to become a doctor from an early age and had never wavered in her determination. For her, medicine was a true vocation while for him it had been the course he'd followed at university, the one he had pursued largely in order to please parents and teachers who'd sought the kudos of having a doctor in the family or on the school records.

He had gone all the way through medical school before maturing enough and achieving the self-confidence necessary to admit to himself and everyone else that he had no great wish to board the medical career train: his heart simply wasn't in it. When the arguments were over and the dust had settled he had gone on to complete his studies and qualify as a doctor, even working his obligatory registration year in hospitals before veering off to join the army and pursue a career more suited to his love of the outdoors and a yen for adventure.

A strong build and a natural athletic ability honed on the mountains of his native Cumbria had ensured rapid progress in the military, serving with the Parachute Regiment and then with Special Forces in operations all over the world. The army, of course, did not ignore his medical qualifications and had put them to good use in training him up to become an expert in field medicine, the medicine of the battlefield where initiative and the ability to improvise were often as important as professional knowledge. It was these qualities that would later lead to his recruitment to the Sci-Med Inspectorate when the time came for him to leave the service in his mid-thirties.

The Sci-Med Inspectorate comprised a small investigative unit based in the UK's Home Office under the direction of Sir John Macmillan. It was their job to investigate possible crime or wrong-doing in the hi-tech areas of science and medicine – areas where the police lacked expertise. The investigators were all qualified medics or scientists who had done well in other jobs before coming to Sci-Med. Macmillan did not employ new graduates: his people had to have proved themselves under stressful, demanding condi-tions in real life. Turning out for the local rugby club or indulging in executive team-building games at the weekend did not count for much to his way of thinking. He knew the most unlikely people could crack when reality came to call.

Steven had proved himself to be a first class investigator and was regarded as such by Macmillan although they had not always seen eye to eye, Steven often feeling frustrated when highly placed wrong-doers were too frequently in his eyes allowed to get away with their crimes in the so-called 'national interest'. A couple of years before, things had come to a head after a particularly diffi-cult assignment and Steven had resigned from the Inspectorate to begin a new life with Tally – Dr Natalie Simmons – a paediatri-cian working in a children's hospital in Leicester whom he had met in the course of a previous investigation.

Tally had never really come to terms with what Steven did for a living, having witnessed at first hand some of the dangerous situations he found himself in. It had proved such a stumbling block to their relationship that they had parted over it, with Tally declaring that she couldn't face a life of continual worries over whether her man was going to come home or not. Things had changed when Steven resigned from Sci-Med and got back in touch to tell her so, assuring her that he had no intention of returning. Would she now consider spending her life with him? To his relief, Tally's feelings hadn't changed. She had welcomed him back with open arms.

Steven had found a job with a large pharmaceutical company in Leicester as head of security – more concerned with the guarding of intellectual property and the vetting of staff than the patrolling of premises – and they had set up home together in Tally's flat. Despite loathing his job and finding himself in the rat race he'd always managed to avoid, Steven declined all attempts by John Macmillan to lure him back to Sci-Med, believing that, in time, he would grow to feel better about his new career and consoling himself with the thought that at least he had Tally.

An unexpected wildcard had been thrown into the mix when Macmillan had fallen ill with a brain tumour and had asked to see Steven before undergoing major surgery with what doctors had warned him was a less than certain outcome. At Tally's insistence, Steven had travelled to London to be at Macmillan's bedside, only to find himself immediately under pressure when Macmillan asked that he seriously consider taking over from him as head of Sci-Med should he fail to pull through. Steven, faced with the awful choice between reneging on his promise to Tally and turning down a possible last request from the man he respected more than anyone else, had in fact declined. He had apologised to Macmillan, hoping that he'd understand how much Tally had come to mean to him and that he couldn't risk losing her.

There was to be another twist, however, when Tally, sensing how unhappy Steven was in his new job – although he'd never openly admitted it – and how badly he fitted in to the system of corporate hierarchy, decided that she couldn't be party to such a situation any longer. She'd insisted that Steven return to Sci-Med: she would support him and they'd work something out.

In the event, Steven did not commit to taking over at Sci-Med but did agree to go back and take a look at something that had been troubling Macmillan greatly, the sudden deaths of a number of people including a former health minister who'd been involved in a series of health service reforms some twenty years before. It was during the course of this investigation that Macmillan underwent surgery and amazed his doctors by making a good recovery against all the odds. He was now back at Sci-Med in full charge of all his faculties and the organisation he had founded.

Steven, who had resigned his job with the pharmaceutical company in order to carry out the investigation, was still with Sci-Med but ever mindful of how Tally felt, whatever she said – something that constantly caused him to overstate the routine nature of what he was doing, hoping to convince her that being in danger was very much the exception rather than the rule. Tally didn't really believe it and he had to concede that she did have a point. He had come perilously close to losing his life on more than one occasion in the past few years.

Tally hadn't come with him to Scotland this weekend: she'd agreed to provide cover at the children's hospital for her boss, whose mother had died after a short illness. Steven had driven north alone to spend time with his daughter Jenny and the family she had lived with since his wife Lisa's death. Jenny had been a baby at the time but was now moving into the 'seniors' at her primary school in the village of Glenvane in Dumfriesshire where she lived with Lisa's sister, Sue, her solicitor husband Richard and their own two children Peter and Mary.

Tally and Jenny got on just fine but Steven had given up harbouring dreams about his daughter's coming to live with them on a permanent basis and all of them playing happy families – a notion of domestic bliss he'd entertained for some years, albeit to happen at some unspecified time in the future. He now recognised it as being both impractical and unrealistic. Jenny had lived too long with the folks in Glenvane and was happy there, accepted and much loved as one of the family. Having a 'real daddy' who came to visit whenever he could was a bonus in her life, not an alternative. Sue and Richard had agreed with this assessment, having no wish at all to lose their 'second daughter'.

Apart from this, Tally had a career of her own to pursue and no thoughts of giving it up. In fact, Steven's return to Sci-Med had encouraged her to start applying for a consultant's post, the next step up from her current senior registrar's position and something she'd been delaying because of Steven's having given up so much to come and live with her in Leicester. Success would almost certainly mean a move to another town or city, but with Steven living in London through the week Leicester was no longer their natural base. A position in a London hospital would suit them both down to the ground.

Steven paused in his progress along the water's edge to pick up a handful of stones and begin throwing them out as far as he could, straining to hear the splash against the sound of the wind in his ears. Each successful one seemed to trigger a new thought about Simone. Whereas he had gone off to join the army as soon as he'd finished medical school, Simone had gone off to do what she could for the sick and the suffering in the third world. She would never follow the traditionally comfortable career path of the medic to middle class affluence and status. She would use her skills and dedication to help those who needed her in Africa and Asia throughout a career which had come to an abrupt and unfair end for whatever reason.

She had been working for some years for MSF, prepared to go wherever they chose to send her, but she was also a very charming and persuasive woman who had been used by the organisation to seek funding and practical help from big business – mainly the pharmaceutical industry – on many occasions, something she'd proved good at, with company executives often complaining with good humour that she could pick their pockets without their realising what had happened.

Steven had first met her when he had been seeking information about an outbreak of Ebola in one of the African countries where she had recently been working. He had been trying to identify the source of a possible case being held in a UK isolation unit. They had liked each other from the outset and their friendship had been cemented when Simone spoke of the difficulties of performing surgery in the bush and Steven was able to help her with tips and suggestions gained from his own wide experience of field medicine. Carrying out emergency surgery on the wounded in the deserts of the Middle East and in the depths of the South American jungle had given him a lot to pass on.

Simone could never understand why Steven had joined the army in the first place – *You train to save life and then you train to take it? It's crazy* – just as he didn't understand why she had devoted her entire life to what he saw as taking on an impossible task with the odds continually stacked against her and everyone like her. He was a very practical individual who didn't believe in getting into fights he couldn't win while she was very much an 'It's better to light a candle than curse the darkness' sort of person. Although he'd never said so, Steven had always suspected that religion might be behind Simone's outlook, as was so often the case with those involved in the apparently selfless doing of good, but this idea was torpedoed when on one occasion Simone had volunteered that she didn't believe in God. It had taken him so much by surprise that he could only mumble 'Me neither'.

They had met at irregular intervals, usually when Simone was in London with her 'begging bowl', as she put it, although it sounded better with a French accent. They would get together for dinner and discuss the state of the world, Steven's views reflecting his ever-growing cynicism while an apparently eternal optimism that always made him laugh shone from Simone. He smiled at the memory as he picked up another handful of pebbles to throw into the sea. He had once said to her that he could understand why everyone liked her but failed to see what she saw in him. She'd laughed and put her hand on his arm to reply, 'You have a good heart, Steven. Don't try so hard to hide it.'

TWO

'All right?' asked Sue, who was working in the kitchen when Steven entered by the back door.

'Yes thanks,' Steven replied. 'Sorry about running off.'

'Don't be. It's when the death of a friend doesn't affect you that you should start to worry.'

Steven smiled. 'How come you always know the right thing to say?'

'You obviously weren't at the last meeting of the PTA when I suggested that the collective IQs of the local council wouldn't break three figures.'

'Did you really?' exclaimed Steven, his voice betraying more admiration than shock.

''Fraid so. Maybe you should go talk to Jenny for a bit. She's on the games console with the other two.'

The children were arguing about whose turn it was next when Steven entered the playroom. Jenny rushed over to him and gave his waist a big hug. 'Auntie Sue said you'd had some bad news about one of your friends, Daddy.'

'I'm afraid so, nutkin.'

'Are they dead?' asked Peter, the eldest of the three.

'Yes she is, Peter.'

'Was she a policeman like you, Daddy?' asked Jenny. Sue and Richard had brought her up to believe that this was what Steven did in London.

'No, nutkin, she was a very kind doctor who worked in far-off countries helping sick children.'

'Was she eaten by a lion?' asked Mary.

'Don't think so, Mary.'

'What will the sick children do now?'

'The other doctors will have to do extra work.'

'I'd hate it if one of my friends died,' said Peter, and the other two concurred with nods.

'Maybe we should talk about something else, like what we're going to do tomorrow,' suggested Steven.

'Swimming,' exclaimed Peter.

'Yes, swimming,' echoed the other two.

'Swimming it is then,' said Steven, pleased that the tradition of going swimming at Dumfries pool during his visits was not to be broken, although he suspected that the junk food lunch afterwards followed by as much ice cream as they could handle had more than a little to do with their decision.

With the children in bed and Sue and Richard parked in front of the TV watching a serial they followed, Steven went off to his room to call Tally.

'Having fun?' she asked.

Steven told her about Simone.

'I don't think you've mentioned her before.'

'It's been a couple of years since I last saw her.'

'Was she . . . special?'

'Not in the way you mean, but she was a special sort of person.' Steven told Tally about Simone's work with *Médecins Sans Frontières*.

'So what was it? Guilt or booking a front-row seat in heaven?'

'Neither,' replied Steven, permitting himself a small smile. Tally was nothing if not forthright. 'Simone didn't believe in God and she had nothing to feel guilty about. She told me she had a very happy childhood; sailed through medical school with an armful of prizes before joining Med Sans.'

'Then she really was special,' conceded Tally. 'A truly good person. You don't meet many of those along the way.'

'Yep.'

'So what happened?'

'John didn't know. He just thought I should be told. He'll call back when he learns more.'

'Are you going to stop off in Leicester before you go back to London?'

'If you'll have me.'

'Oh, I'll have you all right,' murmured Tally.

A broad smile broke out on Steven's face. 'You could make good money with a telephone voice like that.'

'Where d'you think the flat came from?'

'I find out a little more about you each day.'

'I'll have to watch that. Take care, Steven. Sorry about your friend.'

John Macmillan called just after nine thirty. 'It was an accident.'

'What kind?'

'She died in a fall from a gallery in the library of the Strahov monastery in Prague.'

'What?' Steven exclaimed as if it were the last thing he expected to hear.

Macmillan repeated it but added, 'It's not quite as strange as it sounds. She was attending a scientific meeting in Prague and a visit to the monastery was arranged for the delegates. Apparently the monastery library has a particularly beautiful painted ceiling. Dr Ricard was one of those who climbed up to the gallery to get a better look. For some reason she fell and broke her neck.'

'God, how awful,' murmured Steven.

'I understand her body is being returned to Paris tomorrow. Will you be attending the funeral?'

'I'd like to; depends what we've got on, I suppose.'

'Not much at the moment. I was going to ask you to take a look at a hospital in Lancashire where the cardiac death rates were sky high but the situation has resolved itself. The usual reason – an ageing surgeon not realising his faculties had declined and his colleagues being too respectful to tell him.'

'Always a problem,' sighed Steven.

'Well, finally someone plucked up the courage. Anyway, you can let me know what you decide when you get back. When will that be?'

'It was going to be Tuesday but I'll be back on Monday afternoon – see if I can find out a bit more about Simone's death.'

Steven went downstairs and told Sue and Richard what he'd learned.

'Do you want to cancel the swimming tomorrow?' asked Sue.

Steven shook his head. 'I let the kids down today. I'll take them swimming and then we'll go to lunch, but I'll head south after that and stay overnight at Tally's before going back to London on Monday.'

Steven found Tally exhausted when he got to the flat just after eight o'clock and let himself in. His hello was met with a faint mumble of reply. She was sitting in the living room with her feet up and her eyes closed, a glass of white wine on the table beside her as she listened to the BBC proms.

'Did I mention that I hated the NHS?' she asked without opening her eyes.

'Many times,' replied Steven, planting a kiss on the top of her head as he came up behind her chair. 'But you also love being a doctor, remember?'

'That's what makes it so unfair,' Tally grumbled. 'We've got all these bloody managers playing around with charts and numbers and targets and ticking boxes to make it appear that we're doing well when we're not. If they got rid of them and employed a couple more doctors and a few more nurses, we bloody well would be.'

'It's an unfair world,' Steven soothed. 'I take it you've had a busy weekend?'

'There were times when I felt I was working in a refugee camp. We've got to be so careful when we're dealing with kids who've just arrived in the country. It's so easy to miss diseases and conditions you wouldn't expect to turn up in an English children's hospital. You tend to over-compensate by asking the lab to carry out every test under the sun and they get pretty pissed off. We've also got to be on our guard against TB all the time because it's making a comeback, so we send every kid for a chest X-ray and of course the radiographers start getting grumpy.'

'I can see the problem,' Steven sympathised, sitting down opposite her.

Tally opened her eyes and, feeling slightly guilty, looked at Steven sheepishly. 'But my problems are probably nothing compared to what your friend had to face,' she said. 'I'm sorry for being such a moan. I'm losing my sense of proportion. Hungry?'

'I can fix us something.'

'No you won't. You've had a long drive. Why don't you shower and change? I'll heat up a couple of quiches; we can have them with some salad and a whole lot of wine.'

'Sounds good.'

Later, as they sat with coffee on the couch, Steven asked, 'So how big is this TB problem I keep hearing about?'

'Hard to say. Officialdom doesn't want the extent of the problem becoming widely publicised for fear of stoking racial tensions. The kids presenting with TB are almost exclusively Asian and it would be all too easy to have the right wing shouting about English kids being threatened with a killer disease they'd caught from immigrants, so the figures are wrapped up in something which in turn is disguised as something else.'

'Something the Civil Service are good at.'

'Well, it could be a continuing challenge. TB might not be the only thing making a comeback. There are those who predict we're going back to what it was like in the forties and fifties of the last century.' Tally groaned and stretched her arms in the air. 'God, I'm tired.'

'That's not surprising: you haven't had a day off in weeks. We should think seriously about taking a holiday, somewhere nice and sunny where they have blue skies instead of grey.'

'Holidays are for other people, Steven.'

'C'mon. The hospital could get a locum in. Ask your boss about it. This would be a good time, right? Just after you've done him a favour.'

'We'll see.'

'I'm serious. Talk to him tomorrow. You are going in tomorrow?'

'Does the pope wear red socks?'

THREE

Steven was back in London before one o'clock. He parked the Porsche in the underground car park at Marlborough Court and went upstairs to check that the flat was okay before setting off for the Home Office. He and Tally had decided that he should hold on to the property for a while when he moved to Leicester because the housing market was so dire, a decision that had proved fortuitous with his return to Sci-Med. It might well be the flat in Leicester they would be looking to sell if Tally managed to get a consultancy in the capital.

Jean Roberts, John Macmillan's secretary, welcomed him with her usual good humour and asked after Jenny.

'She's growing up far too fast,' complained Steven. 'Seems like only yesterday she was a baby.'

'It's frightening,' agreed Jean. 'My godson's getting married in a few months and I still think of him as a schoolboy with grubby collars and scraped knees.'

John Macmillan, hearing the voices, emerged from his office and invited Steven through. 'Sorry to be the bearer of bad tidings about your friend. Must have put a damper on your weekend.'

'You did the right thing,' Steven assured him. 'I think I will go to the funeral if that's still all right with you?'

'Of course. The computer's been rather quiet for the past week or so.'

Sci-Med had a sophisticated computer system which gathered information about anything unusual happening in the world of science and medicine by scanning all newspapers and relevant magazines and journals for significant articles.

'Mind you, it's been picking up on a strange story about the vilification of researchers working on ME.'

'What's that all about?' Steven asked.

'Apparently sufferers are fed up with the suggestion that there's a psychological element to their condition. They think it supports the yuppie flu argument and brands them as lazy, shiftless, work-shy malingerers. They're particularly incensed that so much government funding is being poured into this aspect of research when they'd prefer the money to go into the hunt for the real cause of the problem as they see it. They're sure it has a biological basis.'

'I thought a virus was identified a couple of years ago?' said Steven.

'A false dawn, I'm afraid. It turned out to be a contamination problem. No one could ever reproduce the reporting team's results.'

'Messy.'

'It's messy all round. Researchers are saying that ME sufferers would rather be thought to be suffering from a serious but unknown viral condition than have any suggestion of mental health problems attached to them. Needless to say, the mental health lobby are not too delighted about that. They claim it perpetuates the stigma attached to mental problems.'

'So what form has the "vilification" been taking?'

'Threatening letters to researchers, paint daubing, broken windows. There's also an accusation doing the rounds that scientists would prefer not to find the virus responsible because that would put them all out of a job. They're accused of being quite happy with the suggestion of a psychological factor because they know that'll go on for ever and go nowhere.'

Steven permitted himself a small smile. He was no great fan of psychiatry. 'Doesn't sound like something we should get involved in,' he said.

'Agreed, but I'll keep an eye on the situation.'

'Any more from Paris?'

'Details of the funeral arrangements came in,' replied Macmillan. 'Jean has them.'

Steven stopped by Jean's desk on the way to his own office and accepted her offer to arrange flights for him. 'It's on Thursday afternoon,' she said. 'Do you want to stay over?'

Steven thought for a moment before agreeing that this might be the best plan. There would probably be people he'd want to speak to.

'Fine, I'll fix accommodation too.'

Steven smiled when he noticed the new nameplate on his office door. It said *Dr Steven Dunbar, Principal Investigator*. He had only recently agreed to have an office to himself. Previously he had spent as little time as possible in Whitehall, preferring instead to use the small Sci-Med library when he was there for any absolutely necessary paperwork and his own flat for going through files relating to any assignment he'd been given. He saw the allocation of a pleasant room and a fancy nameplate as part of Macmillan's strategy to accustom him to permanency.

He stood at the window for a few moments wondering if he was really ready to commit to any such thing. The office could be seen as a first step in coming in from the cold – an end to front line investigation – something that would please Tally but alarmed him. It gave him the same sense of foreboding he'd experienced when faced with leaving the army, but luckily on that occasion Macmillan had come along to save him from ending up in the kind of job he'd just escaped from in the pharmaceutical industry. He moved over to his desk and started going through the mail.

He stopped suddenly when he came to an envelope with a handwritten address on it. It had a Czech Republic stamp on it. He didn't recognise the handwriting but knew it had to be from Simone. The letter was brief and seemed to have been hastily written. It had a small computer memory card stuck to the bottom with Sellotape.

My dear Steven,

I'm at an international meeting in Prague this week to discuss progress in the eradication of polio programme. My team and I

have been working in the Khyber Pakhtunkhwa region of Pakistan and I know it sounds silly but I'm sure there's something very wrong and they won't let me address the meeting. I'm in London next week to meet with Dr Tom North at City College University. I thought I might come and see you? Please keep the memory card safe and I'll explain when I see you.
As ever,
  Simone.

Steven ran the tips of his fingers lightly over the signature. Simone was worried about something and a day later she was dead. Coincidence? Re-reading the letter clearly wasn't helping. He cut the memory card free of the paper and inserted it in his computer. Nothing on it made sense: the contents comprised a series of unrelated letters, numbers and symbols which caused him to give up after a few minutes. His suspicion was that the card had been corrupted by security scans used by airports or the mail service. Fed up with trying to interpret gobbledegook, he took out the card and set up a Google search for Dr Thomas North.

There were a number of Norths listed but he quickly found the one he was looking for – a senior lecturer at City College, a virologist with a special interest in polio, especially the problems patients who survived paralytic polio encountered in later life. Steven remembered reading something about that recently. Arthur C. Clarke, the celebrated science fiction writer, was one such example.

North's research group was profiled on the university website along with its research aims and a substantial academic publications list suggesting that North was a top man in his field. Steven called the number for City College and asked to speak to him. He was put through to North's lab where a young man with a Scandinavian accent said North was in a meeting. Steven left his number and North called him back an hour later.

'Good of you to call back, doctor. My name's Steven Dunbar; I work for the Sci-Med Inspectorate. I was a friend of Simone Ricard.'

'Ah, what happened to Simone was absolutely tragic. If ever there was an example of the good dying young, that was it. Such a lovely person.'

'I understand she was coming to see you this week?'

'Yes, that's right, she was, and now . . . I can still hardly believe it.'

'Will you be attending the funeral, doctor?'

'I'm afraid I can't; I have a prior commitment – one I can't get out of.'

'A pity. I was hoping to have a word. I wonder; do you think I could possibly come over and have a chat with you?'

North hesitated. 'Ye . . . es, but can I ask what this is about? I mean, sorry to be rude but who exactly are you?'

Steven told him. 'I'm interested in the work Simone was doing on polio eradication. She wrote to me about it.'

'I see. Look, at the risk of sounding macabre, Simone was down to come here on Wednesday morning. You could come in her place?'

Steven agreed and arranged to be there at eleven.

He went through and told Macmillan about the letter from Simone with the computer card attached.

Macmillan raised his eyes and sat back in his chair. 'But no actual indication as to what she thought was wrong?'

Steven said not. 'But my curiosity's been aroused. I'll ask our lab boys to take a look at the card.'

Macmillan nodded. 'Perhaps her colleagues will be able to throw some light on things when you see them at the funeral. Mind you, French citizen dying in the Czech Republic with a UK investigator asking questions . . . Could be the overture to a bureaucratic nightmare if you get too involved.'

Steven acknowledged with a grimace. 'I've also arranged to see the scientist she'd set up a meeting with in London. Maybe he'll have some idea what she was worried about.'

'Was he at the Prague meeting?'

'I'll find out on Wednesday.'

* * *

30

Steven, wearing a dark blue suit and Parachute Regiment tie, told the man in uniform behind the desk whom he'd come to see.

'And what company shall I say *you're* from?' asked the man, barely disguising a sneer and clearly assuming that anyone found wearing a suit in City College must be a sales rep and therefore worthy of derision.

'The Home Office,' replied Steven, placing his ID down in front of him.

The man looked up to find Steven looking through him. It spoke volumes.

'Right sir, sorry sir. I'll let them upstairs know you're here. Perhaps you'd care to take a seat over there?'

A few minutes later a young man wearing jeans and a checked shirt appeared from one of the lifts. He had an engaging if lopsided smile and a shock of curly red hair. When he spoke it was with an Irish accent. 'Dr Dunbar? I'm Liam Kelly. Tom's expecting you. I'll take you up to the lab.'

'You're one of Dr North's people?'

'PhD student, just about to start my second year.'

'Working on?'

'Virus survival strategies.'

'I'm imagining a dozen virus particles sitting round a table making plans for the future,' said Steven.

'I'd like to be a fly on the wall at that meeting.' Liam laughed as the lift doors opened. 'It would save me a whole bunch of work.'

He led the way through swing doors into a brightly lit lab with a number of people at work in it. All seemed intent on what they were doing as familiar lab smells from long ago of solvents and Bunsen burner-heated air assaulted Steven's nostrils. Thomas North's office was one of two adjoining rooms at the head of the lab. Liam knocked and put his head round the door. 'Dr Dunbar is here.'

FOUR

North turned out to be a tall, bearded, gangly man in his late thirties – a typical academic, Steven thought, from the open-necked checked shirt under the horizontally striped jersey to the corduroy trousers and casual boat shoes. His handshake was firm but Steven noticed that his knuckles were showing early signs of arthritis.

'Good of you to see me,' said Steven.

'A pity it's under such tragic circumstances,' said North with a sigh. 'Did you know Simone well?'

'We'd been friends for some years,' Steven replied. 'You?'

'I met her a few years ago at a polio conference in Geneva. She seemed a very dedicated woman.'

Steven nodded. 'She was. Did you attend the meeting in Prague?'

'Yes. I was there with one of my group but she and I didn't have much time to talk. I think it was for that reason that she asked if she could come and see me in London. Apparently she was coming here anyway to see a couple of pharmaceutical companies about upping their support for the vaccination effort in Afghanistan.'

Steven smiled. 'Sounds like Simone. Can I be rude and ask what exactly she was coming to see you about?'

'She didn't actually say but I suppose she didn't have to. She's been working for some time on the eradication of polio programme supported by the World Health Organisation and we're an international reference lab for polio and vaccine development. It's quite normal for scientists and workers in the field to meet and exchange information. Sometimes things that work well in the lab don't translate to the real world, so reports from the field are valuable.'

'But you're a British lab.'

'And she was French,' said North, seeing it coming. 'Don't read too much into that. The outfit Simone worked for, *Médecins Sans Frontières*, prides itself on being independent and international. Apart from that, labs working on polio are not too thick on the ground these days.'

'And you are one of the best?'

'We like to think so,' North said with a modest smile.

'Tell me, in the brief time you saw her in Prague, did Simone seem upset at all about anything?'

'Upset?' North thought for a moment. 'More frustrated than upset, I think. She wanted to address the meeting but seemed to think the meeting organisers were avoiding her.'

'Were they?'

'I really couldn't say,' said North. 'Meeting organisers are always under a lot of pressure from people wanting to speak, especially when things aren't going too well and everyone has a theory. They have tough decisions to make.'

'The Prague meeting was solely about eradicating polio?'

'It was,' agreed North. 'Or more correctly why that hasn't happened.'

Steven raised his eyebrows and North continued. 'Ever since the WHO eradicated smallpox from the planet, it's been the ambition of the organisation to do the same with polio. A multinational body with the grand title of the Global Polio Eradication Initiative was set up but achieving its goal has been proving more problematical than anyone imagined. The original target for eradication set in 1998 was the year 2000 but that wasn't met. A new target was set for 2005 but that came and went too so they gave up on targets.'

'So how are things going in 2011?' asked Steven.

'Not that well,' admitted North with a grimace. 'That's really why the Prague meeting was called.'

33

'So what d'you think the problem is?'

'It's not just the disease we're fighting in the countries where polio is still hanging on. We have extreme geography and equally extreme politics to contend with as well. The situation in northern Nigeria where the predominantly Muslim population are very suspicious of vaccines from the west interferes with vaccination programmes, and the ever-changing situation in Pakistan is a factor too, not to mention the inaccessibility of the Afghan/Pakistan border regions with their mountain passes and remote villages. Apart from that – and this is a personal hobby horse – I think it actually might not be possible to completely wipe out polio simply because of the vaccine they're using.'

'The vaccine?'

'They're using a live virus vaccine. It's polio virus that has been attenuated so it can't cause polio any more but will elicit the same immune response and cause the body to produce antibodies which will be effective against the real thing. It has the added convenience that it can be given on a sugar lump.'

'I think I had that,' said Steven. 'Are you suggesting it's not effective?'

'Oh, no, it's very effective.'

'Then . . . ?'

'I suppose it's an academic point,' North conceded, 'but the fact remains that polio virus can't be considered completely wiped out if it lives on inside you . . . even if in an altered form.'

'I see,' said Steven, silently thinking that it did seem to be an academic point but feeling obliged to ask, 'I take it there's no alternative?'

'Yes there is. There is a vaccine containing a completely inactivated form of the virus – all the virus particles are dead – but it has to be given by injection.'

'So why not use that?'

North smiled. 'Money, doctor, money, the bottom line to so much these days. We're talking about maybe wiping out the last one per cent of the disease on earth. Pharmaceutical companies are commercial concerns. They exist to make money. The inactivated vaccine is very expensive to make and is in short supply. Governments in places like Pakistan, Afghanistan, Nigeria and India don't want to spend money they don't have to and the pharmaceutical companies don't really want to make it because none of them wants to set up a hugely expensive production line to manufacture a vaccine which will kill off demand for itself almost as soon as it's put into use.'

Steven let out a long sigh as he saw the problem.

'You can't really blame these countries for continuing to use the cheap vaccine to rid themselves of the immediate problem of polio without thinking too much about the finer points of epidemiology,' said North.

'Are there any countries in the world where polio is a major problem?' asked Steven.

'No,' North admitted. 'Cases of paralytic polio are currently running at one per cent of the numbers we saw in 1998.'

'So . . .' began Steven, feeling slightly embarrassed and wondering if he'd missed something.

North smiled and said, 'It's all right, I'm used to scepticism. There are those who see the complete eradication initiative as an academic exercise, an ego trip to wipe out a disease which to all intents and purposes is extinct as it is. The sugar lump vaccine has I admit reduced the occurrence of polio to a mere trickle of cases a year.'

'I suppose I can understand their point of view,' Steven confessed, 'I mean given the financial mess we're all in.'

North nodded in resignation. 'Indeed. It's hard to argue the case for a complete wipe-out, but the fact remains that, with a reservoir of the disease still out there, it can always make a comeback. It may be confined to just a few countries at the moment but they are troubled countries and internal strife encourages population movement. When people start hitting the road it's not only their belongings they carry with them.'

'Immigrants and refugees . . .' murmured Steven, thinking

about his earlier conversation with Tally about TB making a comeback. 'Where did Simone Ricard fit into all this?'

'She'd been working with the Med Sans vaccination team in the Pakistan/Afghanistan border region, one of the real remaining problem areas. It's been a really tough nut to crack.'

'Do you have any idea at all what she wanted so badly to talk about at the meeting?'

'I'm afraid not. As I said, we didn't really have a chance to speak and I didn't even go on the trip to the Strahov monastery with the others where we might have had an opportunity to talk.'

Steven nodded, then changed the subject. 'Your research group, doctor; do they all work on polio?'

North clearly didn't see what Steven was getting at. 'I suppose . . .' he said uncertainly. 'Various aspects.'

Steven appeared apologetic. 'I suppose I was wondering why a research group in London was working on polio when it really isn't a problem any more in the western world – I'm assuming that you get traditional funding from the UK research councils?'

'Ah, I see,' said North with a smile. 'Well, yes, we have funding from the Medical Research Council and the Wellcome Trust and one of our students is supported by a pharmaceutical company, so I suppose you could call that "traditional". But we don't actually spend all our time on polio virus although there is a connection. Our main interest is in the persistence of certain viruses in the body. You know – if you get a cold sore on your lip when you're a child the sore will clear up but the herpes simplex virus which caused it will always be with you, lying low if you like, waiting for the time when the conditions are right and then you'll get a cold sore again, whether by exposure to UV light or perhaps through stress or worry; anything that causes a dip in your defences.'

Steven nodded.

'Varicella, the virus that gives you chickenpox, is another. You get chickenpox as a child and you recover but the virus remains inside you until one day in later life you wake up with shingles – same virus, different condition.'

'Ah, I see,' said Steven. 'Interesting.'

'There's also a condition called post-polio syndrome which really intrigues us. It's a problem that survivors from paralytic polio develop in later life – sometimes as much as thirty years after the event. It's very debilitating but has a tendency to be pushed under the carpet by the medical profession because they're embarrassed by not knowing what's going on. We're not embarrassed; we're intrigued. We'd love to know what's going on and not just with those patients. You see, not everyone who gets infected with polio virus itself develops the paralytic disease. Only one in two hundred does. We'd like to know why that is and what the virus actually does in those people who apparently remain well.'

'Fascinating.'

'And of course,' added North with a smile, 'the more you know about your enemy the better. If we understood viruses better it should be possible to design better vaccines. They're still really our only line of defence against viral disease.'

Steven nodded, feeling grateful for the refresher course. 'Thank you for that.'

'Would you like to meet the team?'

'I'd love to.'

Steven was shown round the lab by North, who introduced his group individually and invited them to tell Steven briefly what they were doing – something they did with varying degrees of eloquence. Liam Kelly proved to be the clearest, showing an infectious enthusiasm for his subject, while others were more reticent.

They stopped beside a tall, broad-shouldered man in his early thirties, wearing a T-shirt proclaiming allegiance to an American football team. 'This is my senior post-doc, Dr Dan Hausman,' said North. 'Dan is being supported by Reeman Losch, an American pharmaceutical company. He's working on post-polio syndrome . . .'

Steven smiled and nodded to Hausman before following North along to the next bench. 'Jenny Davis is uncovering the secrets of the herpes simplex virus.'

'I wish,' said an attractive blonde girl, pausing, automatic pipette in hand, to smile at Steven. 'It's like playing hide and seek in thick fog.'

'Well, I wish you luck,' said Steven. 'In fact, I wish you all the very best of luck,' he said, looking up the length of the lab. Turning back to North, he added, 'Thanks for your help . . . and the tour. I feel I know a whole lot more than I did earlier.'

'I hope everything goes well at the funeral tomorrow,' said North. 'Simone was a special person.'

FIVE

Steven felt glad that he'd come to Simone's funeral. He'd been assuming that he would be an anonymous face among hundreds of mourners but that wasn't the case: there were fewer than fifty people there. Although this puzzled him at first it made sense when he thought it through. Simone didn't have a social life; she did not have a wide circle of friends. She had spent her entire working life abroad among the sick and dying of other countries. Those who had known and loved her in these far-off places were in no position to come to Paris to mourn her death. Apart from family members who comprised less than a dozen, Steven reckoned, the mourners were mainly colleagues and administrators from *Médecins Sans Frontières* with perhaps a few representatives from other aid agencies.

Simone's father, a stooped, elderly man with a head of fine, pure white hair that seemed to respond to the merest suggestion of movement in the air, spoke of a wonderful, loving daughter who had always had a good heart. Her boss spoke of an inspiration to others and the very embodiment of all that was good in the medical profession. Steven felt that the third person to speak, a friend from medical school days, hit the nail on the head when she said that Simone – much as she loved her – had always made her feel inadequate. Everyone agreed that planet Earth was a poorer place for having lost Simone Ricard.

Because the funeral was being held in Paris and not Marseilles where Simone's parents still lived, the reception afterwards was held in a small hotel on Boulevard St-Marcel. Steven introduced himself to Simone's father, not expecting him to have heard of him, so he was surprised when Jacques Ricard exclaimed, 'The English soldier? Simone spoke of you. I think you may be the only soldier my daughter ever approved of.'

Steven felt pleased – absurdly pleased; even vulnerable, like a ten-year-old hearing universal praise for the first time. He shook Ricard's hand and nodded, indicating sympathy and thanks together, then turned to the MSF man who had spoken at the funeral, hoping that he might point him in the direction of people who had served with Simone in Afghanistan or had been at the Prague meeting. He was directed towards Dr Aline Lagarde, who he learned had been working with Simone on the anti-polio drive in the Afghan border region, and went over to introduced himself. She was a dark-haired woman in her thirties wearing an elegant black trouser suit over a lilac blouse which seemed to complement the striking colour of her eyes.

'Ah yes, Dr Dunbar. Simone spoke of you many times.'

After opening exchanges about the awfulness of what had happened Steven encouraged Aline to tell him about the work that she and Simone had been engaged in. He had always been a good listener and this had served him well in past investigations. Experience had taught him that you could learn a lot about people by keeping your mouth shut and your ears open. In this case, he had to decide whether or not to mention the letter he'd had from Simone, and it did not take him long to conclude that Aline Lagarde was an intelligent, caring woman who he felt could be trusted to be discreet. He told her about the letter and asked if she had any idea what Simone had meant by saying something was very wrong.

'The letter was sent from Prague?' Aline queried.

Steven felt she'd asked the question in order to give herself time to think through her reply. 'Yes.'

'Simone had . . . concerns.'

'Shared by you?'

'You could say that.' Aline seemed nervous. She considered for a long moment before going on, 'Simone was unhappy about our region being one of the big stumbling blocks in the bid to eradicate polio. We had more cases than anywhere else in the past year. I think she was afraid that people might see it as our fault.'

'But the Afghan/Pakistan border is a huge area; the logistical problems must be tremendous,' said Steven.

'Exactly,' Aline agreed. 'I kept telling her that. We're also talking about the FATA.' She answered Steven's questioning glance with, 'The federally administered tribal areas. It's a wild, lawless region, a bit like the old wild west.'

'Only east,' said Steven with a smile. 'But surely you can't be the only aid agency working in the area?'

'No, of course not; several other agencies are represented there . . . That's sometimes the root of the problem.'

'Really?' Steven probed.

Aline looked as if she had no real wish to continue but Steven's unflinching gaze persuaded her to continue. 'People like to imagine that aid agencies work together in perfect harmony, but people are people. Apart from the inevitable petty arguments and jealousies which always crop up in every walk of life, government approval and cooperation tends to vary with the country of origin of the team involved. Let's say, some agencies are more welcome than others in Pakistan and Afghanistan.'

'I hadn't considered that angle.'

'Simone always tried to rise above such difficulties. "Forget the politics and think of the children" was her mantra. She did her best to build bridges between us and the other agencies where possible and hated the very idea of having to observe strict geographical boundaries when it came to helping children.'

'Who sets the boundaries?'

'It's agreed at government level. Aid agencies have assigned territories to work in. I suppose the idea is to stretch the aid as far as it'll go and avoid overlap.'

'Makes sense, I suppose.'

'It would if we were all working on a flat plain with everything marked out in grid squares,' agreed Aline, showing a feistiness that had previously been kept under wraps. 'But the border country between Pakistan and Afghanistan is not like that. We are talking mountain passes and deep valleys and lots of uncharted areas where, if you come across a village, your instinct is to help, not wonder if it's in your allotted territory or not.'

'But surely everyone understands that?' said Steven.

'You'd be surprised. We came across a village recently where many people were ill, including children. According to the elders, an aid team had been to the village once to vaccinate the children and give out medicine but hadn't come back. Simone got in touch with the relevant agency to ask about vaccine scheduling and was told to butt out. They said it was none of her business and she should stick to her own region.'

'Crazy,' said Steven. 'And did you?'

'No, Simone was furious. We collected blood samples from the sick for lab analysis and gave the children their second dose of vaccine. It was her intention that we should return to that village after she got back from London.'

'Was that the sort of thing that Simone wanted to bring up at the Prague meeting?'

'I think it may have been,' replied Aline uncertainly.

Steven thought it strange that Aline didn't know what her colleague had intended to talk about. 'What made Simone decide to attend the meeting?' he asked.

'I don't know. She didn't tell me she was going,' said Aline with more than a hint of embarrassment. 'I think it must have been a last-minute decision. As far as I knew she was actually on her way to London to seek more funding from big business. I suppose she must have thought it was a good opportunity to get a look at the bigger picture surrounding polio eradication.'

'And maybe vent her frustrations to some of the head honchos about the bureaucratic problems you were having?'

Aline smiled. 'That too. Simone said you were a clever, resourceful man. She said you'd been a tremendous help in giving advice about treating people under difficult field conditions. She passed the expertise on to the rest of us but always gave you credit.'

'That sounds like Simone,' said Steven. 'She always did the right thing.'

Aline laughed. 'That's exactly what she said about you.'

Steven and Aline exchanged contact details and agreed to keep in touch before Steven went off in search of the organiser of the Prague meeting, who he had learned earlier was Dr Thomas Schultz of the World Health Organisation. Schultz, a small, gnome-like man with grizzled features wearing a rough tweed suit was standing, head bowed, staring at the floor as another, taller man spoke insistently into his left ear while waving his arms around to accentuate whatever point he was making. Although Schultz appeared to be listening intently, Steven noticed his eyes dart to the side from time to time as if searching for an escape route.

He was wondering how to interrupt proceedings when he sensed someone at his shoulder and turned to find Aline there. 'You'd like to speak to Schultz?' she asked. Steven agreed that he would. 'That's Edelman monopolising him, Charles Edelman, an American who oversees the spending of US government money in their international aid programme. I'll try to give you a window . . .'

Steven watched as Aline approached Schultz and Edelman and heard her exclaim, 'Dr Edelman! I haven't seen you for ages, not since the meeting in . . . where was it? Berlin, two years ago?'

As Edelman turned towards Aline, she expertly took his elbow and edged him away, offering smiling excuses to Schultz. Steven took his cue and moved in to introduce himself to Schultz, saying that he'd been a friend of Simone's. They exchanged a few words about the sadness of her death before Steven said, 'I understand Simone wanted to speak at the Prague meeting, doctor?'

Schultz nodded but seemed uncomfortable with the question. He cleared his throat unnecessarily and said, 'She made a late request but we have a very tight schedule to stick to at these meetings. It was difficult to fit her in. These things have to be decided months in advance.'

'I take it you know what she wanted to speak about?'

'She had something to say about territorial problems between the various aid organisations in the region she was working in.'

'But you weren't keen on letting her do that?' Steven ventured. It was a gamble, based on what Tom North had said about Simone thinking the meeting organisers were trying to avoid her.

Schultz sighed. 'I have a difficult job, Dr Dunbar,' he said. 'What I strive to do is maintain harmony between the various volunteer groups. Having someone from one group stand up and criticise another at an international meeting was not going to help matters so you could say I wasn't too keen, yes.'

Steven nodded. 'It can't be easy . . . but I understand that Simone's complaint wasn't just about territorial concerns. She believed that another agency wasn't doing its job properly . . .'

'I really couldn't comment. I have no knowledge of that and rumours along those lines could be most damaging to our common cause.'

Steven thanked Schultz politely for his time, and the WHO man was about to move away when Steven added, 'Do you think I could have a list of the people who attended the meeting, and their affiliations?'

Schultz's demeanour changed. He turned with an angry look on his face. 'May I ask why?'

'I might want to talk to some of them.'

'May I ask exactly who you are?' asked Schultz coldly.

Steven told him and gave him his card.

'And what jurisdiction do you imagine you have here?'

'None at all,' replied Steven. 'Do I need it? Surely a list of people attending a scientific meeting can hardly be confidential?'

Schultz's expression suggested he was struggling to keep his temper in check. 'I'll see that one is sent to you.'

'Would it also be possible to have a list of the people who went on the trip to the Strahov monastery too?'

Schultz sighed, then said, 'That was arranged locally. You can ask Dr Mazarek, who is standing over there.' He pointed. 'He made the local arrangements. He'll be able to help you.'

Steven looked to the tall fair-haired man indicated by Schultz. He was in conversation with Simone's parents.

'What exactly is it you're investigating, Dr Dunbar?' asked Schultz.

'I'd just like to know a bit more about the circumstances surrounding Simone's death, doctor.'

'It was a tragic accident. What more is there to know?'

'Probably nothing, I'm sure.'

'You give me the impression you're looking for some kind of scandal, and that is something which could damage the cause that Simone fought so hard for. Any rumour – however unfounded – that her death was anything other than an accident and . . . well, I'm sure you know what the press would make of it.'

Steven nodded. 'Believe me, Dr Schultz, damaging the cause that you and so many organisations work for is the last thing on earth I'd want to do. On the other hand . . . Simone Ricard was my friend. If she had concerns, I'm sure they were well founded.' Steven ended his comment with a hard stare that made Schultz break eye contact, and turned away.

SIX

Steven waited for a chance to speak to Mazarek. When it arose he found the tall Czech to be friendly and outgoing, the kind of person who wore his heart on his sleeve and the sort Steven usually liked instinctively. He said who he was and made polite conversation about how awful it all was before making his request for the list.

The smile faded from Mazarek's face and he looked worried. 'Is there some problem?' he asked.

Steven shook his head and said, 'I'd just like to be clear about everything in my own mind. Call me a compulsive investigator. Come to think of it, was there an official police investigation into Simone's death?'

Mazarek spread his hands and seemed slightly nonplussed. 'Well, the police attended, of course, but we all knew what had happened. Normally visitors to the Strahov are not allowed up into the high gallery, but with it being a private showing for the delegates the rules were relaxed so that people could get a better look at the paintings on the library ceiling. Unfortunately Simone must have leaned out too far, so that she overbalanced and fell to her death; an absolute tragedy. Everyone loved Simone. Surely you can't be suggesting anything else, doctor?'

Steven gave a dismissive shrug. 'No, I loved her too. I'd just like to have a clear picture in my mind of what happened . . . Was anyone with her in the gallery when she fell?'

Mazarek said. 'Lots of people were up there at the time but I think only two saw what actually happened – I guess they were all looking up at the ceiling. But Bill Andrews, an American administrator, and Dr Ranjit Khan, a Pakistani aid worker working in the Afghan tribal areas, were next to her when it happened: they were inconsolable. Bill needed sedation he was so upset. He blamed himself because Simone had been laughing at some joke he'd made just before she lost her balance.'

'I can only imagine how he must have felt. Is Mr Andrews here?'

Mazarek looked around. 'I saw him a few minutes ago.'

'Maybe I'll have a word if I come across him.' Steven smiled and offered his hand. 'Thank you for your help, Dr Mazarek. Oh, sorry, one more thing. You said Bill Andrews was an American administrator. What exactly does he do?'

'He's a field coordinator, doctor, one of the people responsible for the funding and setting up of vaccination programmes on behalf of several US charities.'

'The same sort of job as Charles Edelman?' asked Steven.

'Yes,' agreed Mazarek, 'except that Edelman is responsible for distributing *official* US government money.'

Steven wandered off in search of Andrews, thinking that an American accent shouldn't be too hard to pick up in present company. He found it coming from a man in his thirties who was talking to Aline. Steven thought that he not only sounded American, he looked it too, the clean-cut product of an Ivy League university. He smiled at Aline and she ushered him into the conversation. 'Have you met Bill Andrews, Steven?'

'I was actually hoping we might have a word,' Steven confessed, shaking hands with Andrews as Aline excused herself. 'Dr Mazarek tells me you were with Simone when the accident happened. It must have been awful.'

'God, it's a moment I'll never forget. Hell, I'd just made some stupid joke and I could hear Simone laughing. She must have been looking up at the time and I guess she couldn't have realised how close to the parapet she was. She . . .' Andrews paused as if to compose himself, 'I guess she just toppled over. God, if only I could wind the clock back. The Pakistani doctor who was with us – Dr Khan, I think his name was – and I rushed down the stairs but there was nothing to be done. Simone was dead.'

'What a nightmare for all concerned.'

'I know it's an awful cliché, but Simone was . . . simply the best.'

Steven nodded. 'I wonder, is Dr Khan here today?'

Andrews looked apologetic. 'No, he had to return to Pakistan right after the Prague meeting. Time off is a bit of a luxury for these guys.'

'Of course.'

Someone entering the room caught Andrews' eye and he put his hand on Steven's shoulder and said, 'If you'll excuse me, doctor. There's someone I must speak to while I have the chance . . .'

Seeing that he was adrift and on his own again, Aline joined Steven a few minutes later and he thanked her for getting rid of Edelman earlier. 'It was a bit of luck you knowing him.'

'I don't,' said Aline. 'I'd seen him at meetings, of course, but I'd never actually met him before.'

Steven gave her an admiring glance.

'The poor man was terribly embarrassed at having "forgotten" me. Did you find out what you wanted to know from Schultz?'

Steven shrugged. 'I don't think there was much to find out. I think I'd been reading too much into Simone's letter. Schultz knew that Simone was planning to rock the boat by openly criticising another aid agency and I suspect he and his colleagues were probably a bit heavy-handed in denying her the opportunity.'

'WHO doesn't care for internecine strife.'

'Just out of interest, what was the name of the agency that was pi— annoying Simone so much?'

Aline smiled. 'The organisation that was pissing her off was Children First.'

Steven was embarrassed at his slip. 'You speak English very well.'

'My mother's English,' said Aline. 'Children First is funded by Americans although they tend to disguise that as much as possible by using Pakistani associates. Americans are none too popular in the region where we work.'

Steven nodded. 'I never realised getting aid to the needy was so difficult. It sounds like you have to tiptoe through a minefield of political sensibilities.'

'That's about right,' agreed Aline with a smile.

'So, when d'you go back to the minefield?'

'The day after tomorrow. I'll be taking over Simone's role as team leader and a new volunteer medic will join me at the end of next week, but before I go I want to speak to my bosses. I'm not sure if Simone managed to make her concerns known to them. I think I should do it for her just in case.'

'Good for you. You know, I can empathise with the woman at the service who said that Simone made her feel inadequate. I think you folk all make me feel that way.'

'Nonsense, it's just a job we choose to do,' said Aline. 'How about you? Are you flying home tonight?'

'Tomorrow.'

'In that case . . . maybe we could share a meal this evening if you don't have any other plans?'

'No I don't,' Steven confessed. 'That would be nice.' He had picked up on a hesitation in Aline's voice, thinking that she might be about to add something, but nothing came of it. 'I think I saw everyone I wanted to see this afternoon with perhaps the exception of Dr Ranjit Khan, but Bill Andrews was present at the scene and he seemed a reliable witness. Maybe I should have spent more time commiserating with Simone's parents, but having everyone together in the same room was just too good a chance to miss when it came to asking questions.'

'I'm sure Simone would have understood that you were doing it for her. She was lucky to have such a loyal friend. What now? Investigation over?'

'I think so. I feel a bit happier in my own mind.' Once again he got the impression that Aline wanted to say something, and this time she did.

'Steven . . . Perhaps I haven't been completely frank with you about all Simone's concerns. She actually telephoned me from Prague . . .'

She paused, and Steven urged, 'Go on.'

'No, this is not the time or place. It can wait till later.'

'All right,' said Steven. He and Aline exchanged details of where they were staying and agreed to meet later at a restaurant situated midway between them that Aline knew and recommended, the Monsonnier.

Steven decided to walk by the Seine for a bit before returning to his hotel. He felt uncertain about the conclusions he'd reached after what Aline had just said – or rather not said. Everything had been pointing to his having read too much into Simone's letter but now . . . He wished that Aline hadn't left him hanging.

On impulse, he walked out on Pont Neuf and leaned on the parapet to watch the river traffic pass by as he thought things through again. He paused and smiled as a *bateau-mouche* appeared then disappeared under the bridge, leaving a fading calling card of happy voices and piped accordion music. Another load of tourists were living the Paris dream.

Steven acknowledged the possibility that he might be reading too much into Aline's behaviour. It was pretty clear that Simone's assertion that something was very wrong had to do with the sloppiness of another agency in the field and their subsequent rudeness. Even if Aline were to tell him later that it was a bit more than sloppiness – maybe downright incompetence – it would be no big deal in the great scheme of things. Everyone gets hacked off with colleagues from time to time and probably even more so in the stressful situations in which the two agencies were working.

Simone had been annoyed about getting the run-around from the meeting organisers in Prague but it was clear why it had happened. Schultz had been unhappy about her intention to criticise another agency openly and had stopped her by denying her a speaking slot. As for the fatal fall, an American aid worker and a Pakistani doctor had been in the gallery at the time of the fall and had witnessed the event. They were both distraught afterwards and one even blamed himself for having distracted Simone with a joke before she fell.

Steven had to consider why Simone had sent the letter at all. Why had she wanted to see him? The letter hadn't been a simple suggestion that old friends meet up and she would hardly have approached him about the ins and outs of an aid agency squabble, so why had she felt the need to call on the help of an ex-soldier – or an investigator?

The answer wasn't to be found in the sluggish, muddy water of the Seine or on any of the canvases being studiously worked on by artists on the bridge as he sauntered slowly back to the left bank. He returned to his hotel and showered before calling home.

A breathless Tally answered. 'I'm just in,' she said. 'How'd it go?'

'I'm glad I came. There weren't that many people.' Steven explained why he thought this was.

'A pity. Did you find out what was worrying her?'

'It seems that she felt another aid organisation wasn't doing its job properly and she'd decided to blow the whistle on them.'

'So her death coming immediately after the letter was a coincidence?'

'I think so,' Steven agreed. 'Another fine Dunbar conspiracy theory ruined by a nasty little fact.'

'I'm glad to hear it. I suspect Sci-Med are going to be fully occupied with other things pretty soon.'

'Really?'

'We admitted two children from a refugee family a few days ago. The lab haven't confirmed it yet but we think they're suffering from polio.'

Steven let out a low whistle. 'That's a bit of a show-stopper,' he murmured. 'We were only talking about this sort of thing before I left. Where are they from?'

'Afghanistan.'

'That fits. I'm told it's one of the few places where it's still endemic. How bad are the kids?'

'They're both displaying lower limb paralysis. One of them looks as if she might be getting worse. Her breathing's becoming affected and if that happens . . . poor mite.'

'This sounds like a nightmare from the past, the days of iron lungs and all that. Are the press on to it?'

'Not yet.'

'I take it you're under pressure to keep it under wraps?'

'You can say that again. I'm going back to the hospital tonight. An expert is coming up from London to speak to medical and senior nursing staff about the disease and how we should handle things.'

'Not Tom North?'

'The very same. Do you know him?'

Steven told her that he'd been to see North to get a briefing about the work Simone had been engaged in.

'Well, I look forward to seeing you tomorrow when I can tell you all about it. You are coming up?'

'You bet.'

'So what are you going to do with yourself this evening, all alone in the city of romance?'

Steven cleared his throat. 'Actually, I'm having dinner with a young lady.' He closed his eyes, waiting for the expected 'What?' to arrive. It did. He explained who Aline was.

'Well, don't get carried away with her selfless dedication, will you?'

'No chance,' Steven assured her.

SEVEN

Steven arrived at the Monsonnier at five to eight and sipped kir while he waited. At fifteen minutes past, the waiter asked if Monsieur would like another. Steven said not; his friend wouldn't be much longer. At half past he decided that Aline wasn't coming. He apologised, paid for the drink and tipped well before leaving to walk up and down outside for another ten minutes until he felt absolutely sure she wasn't going to turn up.

Aline's hotel was only a five-minute walk away so Steven thought it might be an idea to go there and check that she was all right. He had almost reached the entrance before impulse gave way to consideration and he decided that this might not be a good idea after all. It might look as if he were annoyed that she hadn't turned up and was looking for an explanation when it was a lady's prerogative to change her mind, he seemed to remember from some way-back code of manners. They had exchanged contact details so presumably she would be in touch to explain at some point – or not.

Steven smiled, thinking how pleased Tally would be when he told her his 'date' had stood him up. He smiled again when he considered that Tally was the best thing that had happened to him for years, and then felt the familiar pang of guilt before adding the rider *since Lisa, of course.* He had loved Lisa dearly and their time together had been all too short. Maybe that was the reason why loving someone else still felt as though it had elements of betrayal about it. Silly after ten years but still undeniable.

He was passing a bar when he thought how inviting it looked, typically French with the kind of effortless atmosphere that business people back home tried and failed to emulate by calling their place a bistro, leaving bare boards on the floor and kitting it out with tables and chairs reclaimed from derelict churches. He went inside and ordered *un ballon de rouge*. It was served quickly and efficiently but without comment, making him reflect on the dislike the English had for the French and in particular for Parisians. It was a view he didn't share. He preferred to see their perceived rudeness as sophistication. They spoke when they had something worth saying: they listened when there was something worth hearing. Steven ordered a *sandwich tunisien* and had another glass of wine before deciding on an early night.

In the morning he was on the first flight out of Charles de Gaulle to Heathrow and was sitting in John Macmillan's office by eleven thirty. Jean Roberts brought in coffee and Steven reported briefly about the Paris trip before Macmillan told him about the two cases of polio in Leicester. Steven had to admit he already knew.

'Of course, that's where Dr Simmons works,' said Macmillan. 'I should have remembered. How is she, by the way?'

'Just fine,' replied Steven, once again noting that Macmillan always referred to Tally formally. He wasn't quite sure why but suspected it might be because Sir John saw her as the main obstacle to his agreeing to take over at Sci-Med one day. 'I'll be seeing her later. I hope to get more details.'

'It seems straightforward enough,' said Macmillan, leaning back in the chair, elbows on the arm rests, fingers interlaced in a steeple. 'Recent immigrant family from Afghanistan.'

'Do we know which region?'

Macmillan searched briefly through some papers on his desk. 'North West Frontier country . . . FATA if that means anything to you?'

'Federally administered tribal areas,' said Steven.

'I'm impressed,' said Macmillan. 'I'm told polio is still rife there.'

'Much to the chagrin of the World Health Organisation,' said

Steven. 'I've learned quite a bit about this over the past couple of days.'

'I remember now, that's where Dr Ricard was working. Well, the Leicester situation is something we can't do much about. It's a straightforward case of importing a disease from the wilds of Afghanistan into our multicultural wonderland. God help us all.'

Steven smiled wryly. He was well aware of Macmillan's views on modern Britain. Multiracial was fine, multicultural was the death of all things British and the road to disaster. 'I was thinking . . .' he began.

Macmillan raised his eyebrows.

'Well, I was wondering as things are a bit quiet for us at the moment if I might take some time off. I've been trying to persuade Tally to take a holiday. She's been working so hard that I'm starting to worry about her, and if this polio business should become more than an isolated incident she might not get a chance again for quite a while.'

'Makes sense,' agreed Macmillan. 'It's a while since you had any real time off too apart from the odd weekend here and there. Recharge your batteries, that sort of thing.'

'Thanks, John. I'll work on Tally this evening.'

'Give her my best.'

Steven had a quick mental picture of Tally's face when he passed on Macmillan's regards. She saw him in much the same light as he saw her: a threat.

Steven was already at the flat in Leicester by the time Tally got home. He hugged her and thought how tired she looked but didn't say so. She slumped down in the sofa and swung her feet up on a footstool.

'Would gin and tonic help?' asked Steven.

'You bet,' sighed Tally, reaching behind her to release her hair, which was always tied back for work.

'Coming right up, my lady.'

'That sounds like guilt to me. What did you and the French dolly get up to last night?'

'She didn't turn up,' replied Steven from the kitchen as he got ice from the freezer. 'Are we out of lemons?'

'Haven't been to the supermarket,' Tally replied. 'What d'you mean she didn't turn up?'

'Stood me up. No message. No apology.'

'Must have been the pins I was sticking in that little doll last night,' murmured Tally, eyes closed, her head back as if to survey the ceiling.

Steven smiled as he returned with the drinks. 'Did you ask about time off?'

Tally opened her eyes, made a face and looked guilty.

'You didn't,' Steven accused . . .

'I just can't see how they could manage right now.'

'Tally, you need a break, and if you wait any longer . . .'

'Yes, I know, there just never seems to be a good time. We seem to have an ever growing population in the city who've never had proper medical care in their lives.'

'And now polio's joining in the fun. How's that situation developing?'

'Public Health are hopeful they can contain it. There's no treatment, of course; it's a case of vaccinating all around the epicentre. The British kids have all been vaccinated already, of course, but the immigrants . . . well, that's a different story. Some have, some haven't and in many cases they don't know. But if everyone stays calm and vaccination is carried out in a systematic and methodical way, we should be all right. What we don't need is any sort of panic. Any kind of story breaking about a killer stalking the streets and we're in real trouble. We need people to stay where they are, not start running all over the place.'

Steven sat down beside Tally and put his head back on the couch beside hers. 'You know, what you said just now – *there's no treatment, of course* – you'd think there would be by now.'

'How so?'

'Well, we've known about viruses and studied them for over a hundred years but we still can't treat them. From the common cold to smallpox or polio, we're no more able to cure them than Florence Nightingale was in her day.'

'But we have vaccination.'

'Yes, we can stop people getting the disease, but if they do get it . . . there's zilch we can do about it. When you think about it, antibiotics came along quite quickly for treating bacterial disease: you'd think anti-viral drugs might have progressed much faster than they have. Don't you think?'

'There's Tamiflu.'

'Which is more successful at making money for shareholders than it is for anything else.'

Steven's phone rang before Tally could reply. It was John Macmillan.

'Steven, do you know a Dr Aline Lagarde?'

'Yes, I met her in Paris. She worked with Simone. Why?'

'You're wanted in connection with her murder.'

Steven's exclamation brought Tally to full, sudden wakefulness. She saw him pale as he stammered, 'Her murder?'

'Dr Lagarde was found dead in her hotel room this morning. She'd been strangled. The Paris police have established that she was meeting you last night but you were nowhere to be found.'

'What do they mean nowhere to be found? I'm here where I belong. This is crazy. I was due to have dinner with Aline last night at a restaurant called the Monsonnier but she didn't turn up.'

'So what did you do?'

'I went to a bar, had a couple of drinks and a sandwich, went back to my hotel and had an early night.'

'The French police say they have witnesses who saw you outside Dr Lagarde's hotel.'

Steven rubbed his forehead in frustration. 'Yes, yes,' he said. 'My first thought when I left the restaurant was to go along there to see if she was okay but when I got there I changed my mind.'

'Why?'

'God, I don't know. It's not as if we were friends. Somewhere along the way it occurred to me that she might think I was annoyed about her not showing up when in reality I just wanted to know if she was all right . . . so I didn't actually go into the hotel. I just turned away. You do believe me?'

'Of course,' replied Macmillan. 'But I think you'd better get yourself back to Paris of your own accord before any official requests start coming in.'

'First thing in the morning.'

'Good. I'll tell the French to expect you.'

Steven took down details of where he should report to and ended the call. He turned to face Tally. 'I take it you got the gist of that?'

'Your date last night was murdered. The French police are hunting you down. Do they still use the guillotine in France?'

'Jesus Christ, what a mess. Poor Aline. What kind of a sick bastard would do something like that?'

'I hate to say it, but maybe the same kind as killed Simone Ricard?' suggested Tally tentatively.

Steven stared at her unseeingly for a few moments before reluctantly conceding the possibility. 'Not just a mess, more a complete can of worms.'

'You never said why you were having dinner with her in the first place,' said Tally.

'She suggested it; I agreed. We were both friends of Simone; that was the reason we were in Paris. I was coming back to the UK in the morning, Aline was returning to Pakistan . . . actually she wasn't. At least not right away.' Steven had remembered that she was going to speak to her bosses at *Médecins Sans Frontières*.

'What about?' asked Tally.

'She wasn't sure if Simone had had a chance to speak formally to anyone from *Med Sans* before her death. Apparently Simone and her team had come across a remote village with lots of sick people in it and kids who hadn't had their second dose of polio vaccine when they should have. When Simone contacted the agency officially covering that area, she was told to push off and mind her own business.'

Tally frowned in puzzlement.

'I gather it was a demarcation thing,' said Steven. 'The village wasn't in her designated area.'

'Sounds like they have NHS managers in Pakistan. Mind you, they would have noticed an unticked box in the vaccination schedules . . . For what it's worth, Steven, that doesn't sound like such a big deal to me. I mean oversights are bound to happen in that sort of environment. We're talking Rudyard Kipling country here. The Khyber Pass and all that.'

Steven nodded. 'You don't have to convince me of that, but Aline told me that Simone felt embarrassed that polio was still endemic there. She took it personally so I guess she'd be hyper-sensitive about any shortcomings she came across. She always gave a hundred per cent and expected others to do the same.'

'Even so . . .'

'There may have been something else,' said Steven.

'Like what?'

'Aline was going to tell me that at dinner.'

Tally raised her eyes heavenwards. 'And now you're going to be hell-bent on finding out what it was?'

'I would like to know.'

'Well,' said Tally. 'It would appear that, yet again, I am to be denied the presence of my man because the fight for truth and justice must go on. You really must start wearing your underpants on the outside, Steven.'

'I'm sorry,' said Steven, knowing how weak it sounded. He took Tally in his arms. 'I love you, Dr Simmons. I love you very much.'

'And I you,' murmured Tally. 'Take care. Come back to me.'

EIGHT

Steven sensed that the French police were enjoying his discomfort. He was being interviewed by three officers in a bare room that smelt vaguely of sweat and tobacco.

'You come with impeccable references,' said the senior detective, who had introduced himself as Philippe Le Grice, in charge of the inquiry into the death of Aline Lagarde. 'The British Home Office apparently thinks highly of you.'

Steven acknowledged with a slightly awkward nod.

'Such pleas on your behalf, of course, mean little when affairs of the heart are concerned, where desire can turn to anger in the blink of an eye and with disastrous consequences for all concerned.'

'There was no affair of the heart,' Steven said coldly. 'I'd never met the lady before. We were both attending the funeral of our friend.'

'Ah, yes, Dr Ricard . . . a fatal fall, an unfortunate accident I understand. So here you were in Paris, the city of love . . . on your own . . . staying overnight . . . and you meet Dr Lagarde . . . an extremely attractive woman by all accounts . . .'

'It was nothing like that,' Steven insisted. 'We talked at the funeral and arranged to have a meal together later before I returned to London and she travelled back to Afghanistan. That's all there was to it, and then Aline didn't turn up.'

'Where did you intend having this meal together?'

'The Monsonnier.'

Le Grice looked to his right where a younger man nodded. 'So she didn't turn up; your evening was ruined; you went to her hotel to demand an explanation . . .'

'You were angry,' interjected the man who had verified the Monsonnier booking.

'No, I wasn't.'

'But you did go to her hotel . . .'

'Well, yes, but only to see if she was all right.'

'And was she?'

'I don't know. I didn't go in,' said Steven, conscious of how implausible it sounded in the circumstances.

'Pathetic,' snorted the one remaining officer, who had sat throughout with a sneer on his face. He got to his feet and leaned across the table, his face close enough for Steven to smell the tobacco on his breath. 'Of course you went in and when Dr Lagarde rejected your advances you had your way with her anyway. Then you strangled her and left her like a piece of trash you'd finished with.'

Steven kept calm but he was struggling. 'Are you telling me that Aline Lagarde was raped?' he asked.

'Are you pretending she wasn't?' retorted Le Grice.

'I've no idea,' said Steven angrily. 'This the first time I've heard it mentioned.'

'You're angry, doctor.'

'Damn right I'm angry. I didn't know Aline Lagarde well but from what I saw I liked and respected her. She, like my friend Dr Ricard, was doing an incredibly difficult job – one that I couldn't do – for very little in the way of thanks or reward and she ends up being raped and strangled in the heart of the "civilised" world and the best you and your bozos can do is question me about it.'

Le Grice turned to his colleagues. 'Leave us.'

This was something Steven hadn't expected.

Le Grice offered Steven a cigarette, which Steven declined, then lit one himself, drawing on it deeply before exhaling and making sure the smoke went upwards by protruding his lower lip. At least we've avoided that little cliché, thought Steven.

'Dr Lagarde wasn't raped,' Le Grice said matter-of-factly.

'Then what the hell was that all about?'

'She wasn't robbed . . . and she wasn't strangled.'

Steven's eyes opened wide. 'Are you telling me that she's still alive?' he exclaimed.

'Unfortunately not. She was shot through the back of the head with a nine-millimetre pistol. Her money and her passport were still in the room and there were no signs of sexual assault.'

'A professional hit?'

'All the signs,' agreed Le Grice.

Steven took a few moments to come to terms with the information before asking, 'Why all the play-acting?'

'We couldn't imagine Dr Lagarde coming across too many hit men in her line of work but, by some strange coincidence, she was about to have dinner with a man who might conceivably fit the bill . . .'

Steven screwed up his eyes for a moment, reluctantly accepting the logic. 'I'm hardly that,' he said softly.

'A Sci-Med investigator with a military past including service with British Special Forces.'

'I had nothing to do with Aline's death.'

'No, I know you didn't,' said Le Grice, 'but I had to be sure. You had nothing to do with Dr Ricard's death either; we checked you weren't in Prague at the time of the "accident". Any idea what's going on?'

'None at all.'

'What's Sci-Med's interest?'

'It's personal,' said Steven, 'not official. Simone Ricard was my friend. I felt I owed it to her to make sure her death was accidental. I thought it was and now this happens . . .'

Le Grice smiled distantly. 'Dr Ricard was French but her death is being regarded by the Czech police as an accident so there is no call for us to become involved. Dr Lagarde's death is quite another matter. We will continue to investigate her murder using all means at our disposal, although the involvement of a professional assassin will . . . complicate things.'

Steven nodded his agreement.

'If, however, you intend to maintain your interest, perhaps we might exchange notes . . . cooperate on our findings?'

'Of course,' said Steven, 'although to be honest I don't quite know where to start.'

'Then we are as one already,' said Le Grice, getting up. He offered his hand then gave Steven his card. 'You're free to go, doctor.'

The air tasted sweet: freedom did have a taste, Steven decided as once again he headed towards a river. It made him reflect on how often he did this in London. There was something about flowing water that drew him, something about the continual motion that calmed his mind and helped him think clearly. What he had to decide was if there was anything he should do in Paris before he returned to London. He couldn't think of anything offhand, but this was more a reflection of what little he had to go on than a conviction that there was nothing more to be done here. He needed to think things through logically to be sure, but first he would call Macmillan and Tally.

'So they let you go; must have been the impeccable reference I gave you,' said Macmillan when told of his release.

'Must have been,' agreed Steven. 'We have to talk when I get back. Things aren't what they seem.'

'I feared as much.'

Tally didn't answer her phone and Steven concluded she must still be on duty at the hospital. He left her a text message before returning to river watching.

The spat between Simone and the rival aid organisation had to be his starting point. It didn't seem much but Aline had injected more into the mix by suggesting there might be more to it. If only she'd lived long enough to say what it was. It had been her intention to talk to her bosses at *Médecins Sans Frontières* about it but that was scheduled for the day after she'd been murdered . . . There was a chance, however, that she might have had some sort of conversation with someone at the aid organisation when she called to make the appointment. He needed an address for Med Sans. He used his BlackBerry to establish a web link and Googled it.

Armed with an address in rue Saint-Sabin he flagged down a taxi and was there in under fifteen minutes, asking at the desk for Guy Monfils, the man who had spoken at Simone's funeral. He was invited to wait and used the time to examine the posters on the office walls, something that left him surprised at how large the organisation was: he was quickly disabused of his previous belief that it was primarily French. *Médecins Sans Frontières* had offices in many countries including the UK where it had premises in Saffron Hill in London. He noted that in several countries it was known as Doctors Without Borders, much more prosaic than the French name which rolled so easily off the tongue.

'Dr Dunbar, this is a surprise,' said Monfils, entering the room. 'What brings you back to Paris?'

'Aline Lagarde's murder,' Steven replied briefly.

'Why don't we go through to my office?'

Monfils settled into his chair and invited Steven to do likewise with an outstretched hand. 'I just hope the police catch the swine,' he said. 'We have lost two of our most dedicated workers in the space of two weeks. It's beyond belief.'

'Tragic,' agreed Steven.

'I'd like to think this a social visit, doctor, but I have a feeling it's not. What can I do for you?'

'I had a letter from Simone Ricard just before she died. In it she confided that she felt something was very wrong.'

Monfils appeared to consider for a moment before asking, 'Did she say what?'

'She didn't, and now she's dead . . . as is her colleague Aline Lagarde.'

'But surely this is some awful coincidence? Simone's death was an accident and Aline was murdered by some lunatic the police are currently hunting for.'

'Maybe,' said Steven, remaining expressionless.

'You can't be suggesting a link?'

'Let's say I'm not ruling it out.'

'My God, what possible reason could there be?'

'I was hoping you might help with that. The Pakistan/ Afghanistan border is a wild, untamed place. Is it conceivable that the women might have upset some people there, some gang, some faction that weren't too keen on having foreigners around?'

Monfils spread his hands and pursed his lips as if doubting the suggestion but wanting to find some way of agreeing. 'Aid organisations are always walking on eggshells in such places,' he said, 'and bandits are a continual problem. But surely the scenario you are suggesting might have accounted for their deaths if they'd died out there . . . not in Prague or Paris.'

Steven had to agree. It was unlikely they would have been followed abroad. He changed tack. 'I understand Aline made an appointment to come and see you before she returned to Pakistan.'

'She did,' Monfils agreed.

'Can I ask what about?'

'She was worried Simone might not have made her concerns known to me in Prague.'

NINE

Steven was disappointed. He'd hoped for some new slant. 'You mean that Children First weren't doing a good job?'

'Precisely that. Simone expected the best from everyone where children's lives were concerned.'

'But no one wanted her speaking about this at the Prague meeting?'

Monfils picked up a pen and appeared to scrutinise it closely as he pondered a reply. Eventually, he said, 'Simone approached both Dr Schultz and myself about speaking but we decided there was no need for her to labour the point publicly. Children First is supported by a number of American charities. Americans tend to be very generous – they are by nature a very generous people.'

Steven thought he saw what was coming next and said, 'And any criticism might have upset the cash flow?'

'Worse than that,' said Monfils. 'We are on the brink of something special. All of us working on the eradication of polio have been disappointed by the persistence of the disease in the region where Simone was working, but now money has been found for a massive attack on the problem – American money.'

'Government money?'

Monfils shook his head. 'No, charity money. Money from film stars, pop stars, business magnates, people all coming together to wipe out this awful disease for once and for all. It hasn't been publicly announced yet but it's going to happen soon. There will be a rapid expansion of aid teams in the area and cash made available for the latest, most effective vaccine.'

'Sounds wonderful.'

'The money, of course, will be channelled through American aid teams.'

'Like Children First,' said Steven, suddenly seeing where Monfils was leading.

'It is, of course, perfectly understandable that American benefactors would like to see the work being carried out by American teams and credit being given to their country of origin.'

'Only human nature,' Steven agreed. 'It's a pity Simone didn't know about this. It sounds like too big a boat to rock.'

'She did,' said Monfils. 'I told her in confidence in Prague.'

Steven was taken aback. 'So what was her reaction?'

'She went straight to Thomas Schultz and demanded an opportunity to speak to the meeting, saying that it was now more important than ever.'

'Why?'

'She wouldn't say, just that she wanted to make a public statement.'

'And now we'll never know,' said Steven with a sigh. It was becoming clear that there was nothing more to be gained from continuing the conversation. He thanked Monfils for agreeing to see him at such short notice and left for the airport.

John Macmillan rubbed his temples in a circular motion with his fingertips when Steven told him he was convinced that both *Médecins Sans Frontières* women had been murdered. 'I can sense your desire to get involved, Steven,' he said. 'I can even understand it, but the French police are investigating Dr Lagarde's death. Perhaps we should give them some time? They may uncover a link.'

'All the signs are that it was a professional hit, John. Chances are they'll get nowhere, and as for the Czech police, they're satisfied that Simone's death was accidental.'

'We can't be sure it wasn't.'

'My fear is that the police there will be only too happy to accept it was an accident. Murder at an international science meeting would be bad for the conference business. I suspect they didn't question anyone too closely.'

Macmillan took a moment to digest this before saying, 'I seem to remember the accident or otherwise occurred at a private showing of the monastery library to the meeting delegates?'

'It did.'

'Then you do realise you are suggesting that Dr Ricard was killed by one of her own colleagues?'

'Or someone pretending to be one of her colleagues,' argued Steven. 'Not everyone knows everyone at these medical conference things.'

'And motive?' asked Macmillan.

'Someone wanted to stop her speaking at the meeting.'

'And Dr Lagarde?'

'She must have known what Simone knew.'

'But you don't.'

'Not . . . yet?' said Steven, knowing that he was throwing himself on Macmillan's mercy. 'There has to be something more to all this than just a territorial spat.'

'This really isn't a Sci-Med affair, Steven. I don't see how we could justify the cost of an investigation . . .'

Steven knew Macmillan was right but couldn't bring himself to say so.

'Unless of course . . . you can see a way?'

Steven snatched at the lifeline Macmillan had thrown him. 'I was thinking,' he began. '*Médecins Sans Frontières* is not solely a French organisation. It's international. There's a British branch here in London which recruits British doctors and nurses.'

'Doctors Ricard and Lagarde were both French,' Macmillan reminded him.

'But the French police are unable to investigate Simone's death officially.'

'Your point being?'

'Simone and Aline were not just French citizens, they were

members of an international organisation – an organisation which includes the UK. Would it not be possible for us to help a sister organisation investigate the unlawful deaths of two of their people?'

Macmillan smiled. 'You're stretching things, Dunbar, but if as you say there's a branch of the organisation in London I'm willing to approach them, see what they think about your idea. If they don't want to have anything to do with it, it's a straight no from me. Agreed?'

Steven agreed.

'And another thing. If we should get a green light and this should go any further, you do not step on the toes of the French police at any point.'

'We've already reached an agreement.'

Macmillan raised his eyebrows but didn't comment. 'I'll let you know what transpires.'

Steven went to his office and found among his mail the list of participants at the Prague meeting he'd asked Thomas Schultz for, and also the names of the people who went on the library visit from the Czech organiser, Mazarek. He scanned through Schultz's list first, looking for British delegates, and found five including Tom North and his post-doc Dan Hausman. Dr Celia Laing worked at the London School of Hygiene and Tropical Medicine; Dr Clive Rollison worked at Birmingham University. Dr Neville Henson worked at the Microbiological Research Establishment at Porton Down.

This last name and affiliation caused Steven to let out a snort. He supposed there was no reason why a scientist from the government's germ warfare establishment should not be present, but the very idea of microbiological warfare always made his blood run cold. Running his eye down the rest of the list, he noted that the Centers for Disease Control and Prevention at Atlanta, Georgia were also represented at the meeting by a Dr Mel Reznik.

Steven checked his watch and decided there was time to put in a call to Celia Laing before setting off for Leicester. He watched raindrops start to patter against the window as he waited to be transferred from the switchboard: the sound made his heart sink. Driving a low-slung Porsche in rain on the motorway was always a less than joyful experience, a bit akin to swimming underwater in a dirty river.

Celia Laing answered and Steven identified himself. It took him a few moments to become accustomed to the sound of her voice. She spoke as if she had too many teeth in her mouth.

'Dr Laing, I understand you attended the recent polio eradication meeting in Prague?'

'Yes, I did.'

'The organisers arranged a trip for delegates to the Strahov monastery where a tragic accident occurred. Did you go on that trip by any chance?'

'Yes, I did. It was a beautiful place but, as you say, a French aid worker fell to her death from the gallery in the library. It was absolutely horrific.'

'I'm sorry if this sounds insensitive, but did you see it happen?'

'No. That is, I was in the gallery at the time but I didn't see her go over, if that's what you mean.'

'I suppose you'd be admiring the ceiling like the others?'

'Actually no, I was looking down at my feet. Someone had lost a contact lens and we were all too scared to move.'

Steven felt the hairs stand on the back of his neck. 'Was this anywhere near where Dr Ricard fell?'

'Yes, quite near. Why do you ask?'

Steven ignored the question. 'Do you happen to know who it was who lost their contact lens?'

'No, sorry. Why are you asking these things?'

'Just routine, doctor. Thank you for your help . . . Oh, shit,' Steven murmured as he ended the call. 'A diversion.'

'So where do you go from here?' Tally asked, soaping Steven's back. It was ten o'clock; she had only been home for half an hour and Steven had just arrived after a hellish trip up the motorway in heavy rain. They had decided that a warm, relaxing

70

shower was called for and Tally's newly installed wet room was proving ideal.

'Depends what Med Sans in London think about us getting involved when John puts it to them. In the meantime I'll talk to some other folk who were on the library trip and see if I can find out who the contact wearer was.'

'In the meantime . . . you'll do no such thing,' purred Tally, becoming more wide-ranging with her soapy hands. 'Stop thinking about work.'

Steven sighed appreciatively. 'Yes ma'am.'

'Good heavens . . .' said Tally. 'I do believe I'm gaining your attention . . .'

TEN

'You know,' began Tally as they had breakfast together, 'if you're right about this person creating a diversion . . . there must have been two of them, one to create the diversion and one to . . . push your friend over.'

'That's right,' Steven agreed.

'Scary, huh?'

'Crazy. And all because she was going to bad-mouth another organisation? I don't think.'

Tally gave a shrug of resignation and asked, 'Are you going back to London this morning?'

'No, I'll phone around a bit, see if I can pick up anything more about what happened in the gallery.'

'Then I might see you later?'

'Indeed you might,' said Steven. 'There's not much I can do in London until John talks to Med Sans.'

'I'll be off then.' Tally bent down to kiss Steven on the cheek. 'You can do the washing up.'

The outside door clicked shut and Steven sat for a few moments in the silence wondering where all this was leading. It was not a good feeling. All he could see ahead was the wall at the end of a blind alley. The silence became oppressive; he got up and turned on the radio before clearing the table. Justin Webb on the Today programme was interviewing a spokesman on behalf of ME sufferers in the wake of the third attack in recent weeks on the home of a scientist working on the problem.

'Surely you can't condone this behaviour?'

'Of course not. We deplore violence in any form but people are angry at not being taken seriously. ME is a very debilitating condition and the public are being encouraged to believe that it isn't. The government's continual refusal to fund proper research . . .'

'What exactly do you mean by proper research?'

'A properly organised search for the organism responsible for the condition.'

Webb turned to a government spokesman. 'Well, why don't you?'

'Simply because there is no evidence at all that a bacterium or virus is responsible. Many have looked . . .'

'They've played at looking,' interrupted the ME man. 'A few individual scientists coasting along on the grants gravy train, pretending to search and determined to find nothing that would stop the train rolling along . . .'

'You can't seriously suggest that scientists don't want to find the cause,' exclaimed Webb.

'It's ridiculous,' agreed the government man. 'I think it's more a case of ME sufferers being unwilling to face facts . . .'

'Which are?'

'That there is a . . . psychological element to the condition, something that ME sufferers seem dead set against.'

'Because it's baloney,' asserted the ME man. 'The government want to brand us all as indolent layabouts because it's a damned sight cheaper than funding proper research.'

'Gentlemen, I'm afraid the clock has beaten us . . .'

Steven finished putting away the last breakfast plate and turned off the radio before going in search of his briefcase and the Prague meeting lists. He brought back both and sat down at the kitchen table to enjoy the morning sunshine streaming in through the window. A glance at his watch told him that it was too early to start phoning anyone in academia so he made himself an espresso and set about sorting the participants into new lists. The originals were in alphabetical order: he grouped them using different parameters, the first being nationality, the others based on whether they were scientists or medics and whether they were academics or aid workers, and finally sub grouped the aid workers, under the organisations they worked for. By the time he had entered the information into his laptop it was time to make the first phone call.

'The what inspectorate?' asked Clive Rollison at the University of Birmingham.

Steven repeated himself and explained briefly what Sci-Med did. 'I'd like to ask you a few questions about the polio eradication meeting in Prague you attended.'

'I've already explained the oversight to the travel grants committee . . .'

'Nothing like that, doctor. A young woman fell to her death at the meeting.'

'Yes, Simone Ricard. Shame; a nice woman.'

'Were you anywhere near at the time?'

'What is this? Are you suggesting I had something to do with her death?'

'Good heavens no, I just wondered if you saw what happened.'

'I was in the gallery at the time, as it happens, but I didn't actually see it. There was some kind of kerfuffle about somebody losing a contact lens, then there was a scream and all hell broke loose; people were shouting and crying; several rushed downstairs to see if they could help but there was nothing anyone could do. Her neck was broken; I could see that from the angle she was lying at when I looked over the balustrade.'

'How high was the balustrade?'

'Not that high, to be honest. I don't think they normally allow visitors up there and the floor was a bit uneven. I don't think Health and Safety would have passed it here. Mind you . . .'

'Quite. Were you anywhere near the kerfuffle you mentioned?'

'Not really, about twenty metres away I guess. I was looking up at the ceiling and then I heard the commotion and turned round. People were getting down on their hands and knees to look for a contact lens while others were saying, "Don't move, you'll stand on it." There was nothing I could do so I went back to admiring the ceiling and then I heard the scream . . . and the thud.'

Steven decided not to call anyone else for the time being: he was convinced he was just going to hear variations on what he'd already been told. He changed from Mazarek's list to the official meeting register. Simone and Guy Monfils were the only participants from *Médecins Sans Frontières*; there were five people from WHO, including Thomas Schultz the meeting organiser, three from Children First, the organisation Simone had been concerned about, several Americans concerned with funding – both government and charity sourced – and a range of aid workers from Pakistan and Afghanistan. In addition, there were government observers from Nigeria, Pakistan, Afghanistan and India as well as Tom North and Dan Hausman from the North lab in London.

Neither Celia Laing nor Clive Rollison knew who'd lost or claimed to have lost their contact lens but someone had to know. To have been a diversion, the incident would have had to happen close to where Simone was standing, so those nearest her at the time would be most likely to remember who had raised the alarm. Bill Andrews, the American charity administrator, had been nearby; he had been joking with her. He must know.

Steven was looking for contact details for Andrews when his phone rang: it was John Macmillan. 'Where are you, Steven?'

'Leicester. Have you heard back from Med Sans?'

'That's no longer relevant. I need you back here tomorrow morning. We've been summoned to a meeting.'

'At their place?'

'At the Foreign Office.'

Steven was taken completely by surprise. 'Why . . . how . . . ?'

'I dare say we'll find out tomorrow. What are you doing right now?'

Steven told him.

'Better put your investigation on hold for the time being.'

Steven was sitting wondering what on earth Macmillan had said to *Médecins Sans Frontières* to attract the attention of the

Foreign Office when a text message came in from Tally. She apologised but said she'd have to work late. Steven returned the apology saying he'd been summoned back to London. He'd call when he knew more.

The next day Steven arrived at the Home Office just before nine o'clock and asked Jean Roberts, who was taking her coat off in the hall at the time, if she knew what was going on.

'I'm afraid not,' she replied. 'To be honest, I think Sir John is mystified too. It was more of a directive than a request. The pair of you are required to attend at ten a.m. with no indication of what the meeting's about.'

'Someone's been watching too many episodes of *Spooks*,' suggested Steven.

Jean appeared to smile and frown at the same time, an ability that always amused Steven. Jean was very much of the old school when it came to respect for people and protocol. He had never known her make a derogatory comment about anyone working in Whitehall in all the years he'd known her. Quite a feat, he thought, when she was so spoilt for choice. Macmillan arrived and they had coffee in his office before going over to the Foreign Office.

Steven felt more bemused than ever when they entered the meeting room and saw who was there. He could sense that Macmillan shared his surprise as he acknowledged the presence of the Foreign Secretary, the head of MI6, the CIA chief of the London station and Guy Monfils from MSF. There were a few other people there whom he didn't recognise.

Macmillan and he were shown to their places at the table and it immediately became apparent that the meeting had been called for their 'benefit'. Steven felt as if he were about to be interviewed for a job.

'Thank you for joining us, gentlemen,' said the Foreign Secretary with a smile that was intended to lighten the atmosphere. It was not returned by Macmillan or Steven who both remained impassive, thinking they hadn't had much choice in the matter.

'I'm led to believe that in recent weeks Sci-Med have been taking an interest in the tragic death of a *Médecins Sans Frontières* aid worker, Dr Simone Ricard. Is that right?'

'Simone was a friend,' said Steven. 'I'm not entirely convinced her death was accidental.'

The Foreign Secretary took a deep breath as if this were something he had no wish to hear. He continued, 'You attended her funeral in France where you asked questions of several people and gave the impression that you might be continuing your inquiries . . . your admittedly unofficial inquiries.'

'I wanted to know the truth. I still do.'

'And to that end, Sir John has approached MSF here in the UK?'

'I wanted to know what they thought before committing to anything officially,' said Macmillan. 'Is there a problem?'

The Foreign Secretary gave Macmillan a long hard look before replying, 'Sort of.'

ELEVEN

Steven and Macmillan exchanged glances while waiting for the Foreign Secretary to continue.

'You have probably established that Dr Ricard was unhappy about the behaviour of certain of her colleagues in the field. She wanted to speak publicly about this at a meeting in Prague but was denied the opportunity. Your suspicion is that she was murdered in order to keep her quiet about her misgivings. Am I right?'

'There have been two deaths,' Steven reminded him.

'Yes, thank you. Dr Lagarde. I will come to her later. This meeting has been convened to put you both in the picture. Dr Ricard was right to be concerned about the actions of the Children First team she came across and their apparent lack of expertise. I'm afraid – no, embarrassed – to tell you that they were not an aid team at all apart from one Pakistani doctor. They were a CIA intelligence-gathering unit.'

'Masquerading as a medical aid team?' exclaimed Macmillan. 'That's outrageous. It's like using ambulances to cover troop movements. It's just not on.'

'I think the CIA has been made aware of the strength of feeling their actions have generated,' said the Foreign Secretary, turning his head slightly towards the CIA chief.

'Why do it in the first place?'

'Abbottabad,' said the CIA chief, speaking for the first time. 'We were going after Bin Laden: we knew we were getting close but we had to be sure.'

'So you put the health of God knows how many children at risk to get to one man,' said Steven.

'He wasn't just one man, dammit,' snapped the CIA man. 'He was an icon, a figurehead. While he lived, 9/11 would never be avenged in the eyes of the American people. We had to take him out while we had the chance.'

'Had the chance?'

'Intelligence gained by the teams pointed us at the compound at Abbottabad but we still had to be sure Bin Laden was there. One of the vaccination teams gained access to the compound and brought away samples for DNA analysis. They were positive. We sent in the SEALS and the rest . . . you know.'

'Well, that's all right then,' said Steven sourly. 'Polio will remain endemic in the region and the vaccination teams will not be able to stop it because no one will trust them any more but hey, you got your man. John Wayne would have been very pleased.'

Macmillan put a hand on Steven's arm to rein him in.

'I know what we did . . . was perhaps wrong in a moral sense,' began the CIA man, 'but we've apologised to all the aid agencies involved and there is to be a major new initiative in the region funded by American sources . . .'

'To keep everyone quiet,' said Steven.

'Look, we've put our hands up and apologised. I don't see what more we can do.'

One of the people from the World Health Organisation decided to breach the ensuing uncomfortable silence. 'As chance would have it, the international press tended to concentrate on the death of Bin Laden and, of course, the bravery of the military team involved. There was little reported about the use of fake aid teams. For our part, we saw there was nothing to be gained by focusing attention on this aspect so that is why we discouraged Dr Ricard from speaking at the Prague conference. It would have been . . . counter-productive.'

'Dr Ricard's death was an accident,' said the Foreign Secretary. 'There was no plot to keep her quiet.'

'And Aline Lagarde?'

'I'm afraid Dr Lagarde was not all that she seemed. During the course of their investigations the French police have established that she was involved in the transport of heroin from Afghanistan into France. They believe that she grew too ambitious and double-crossed those who were funding her . . . with fatal consequences.'

'Jesus,' murmured Steven.

'Not good news, I'm sure, but I hope we have been able to put your minds at rest with regard to conspiracy theories.'

'Did we know what the CIA were up to in Afghanistan?' Steven asked the MI6 man.

'Bits and pieces,' came the guarded reply.

Steven and Macmillan walked back to the Home Office largely in silence, Steven intent on looking at the wet pavement, Macmillan gazing into the distance like a ship's lookout. It wasn't until they were in the lift that Macmillan asked, 'Well, what d'you think?'

'If Aline Lagarde was a drug runner, I'm about to be appointed principal ballerina with the Bolshoi Ballet.'

'A possibility I'd rather not dwell on,' said Macmillan, 'but I agree. It did all sound terribly . . . unlikely.'

'They definitely don't want us poking around,' said Steven. 'So what are they hiding?'

'On top of everything else, you mean. What the combined intelligence services of the UK and our American cousins are hiding doesn't bear too much thinking about.' They'd reached Macmillan's office. Steven watched while his boss poured two large sherries and handed him one. 'Once again the fickle finger of fate has put us on a collision course with HMG.'

Steven chose to sip his drink rather than reply.

'The question is, what do we do now? The bright thing . . . the clever thing . . . the dutiful thing . . . would be to walk away and leave it. After all, what they're up to in far-off places is hardly a matter for Sci-Med.'

'I'm still convinced Simone and Aline Lagarde were murdered for the same reason,' said Steven.

'I thought you'd see it that way,' said Macmillan, sounding less than overjoyed. 'The odds against our being able to do anything against the combined opposition of MI6, the CIA, and possibly even the French intelligence services if they were responsible for setting Dr Lagarde up, are overwhelming.'

'True,' Steven conceded. 'But that doesn't stop us thinking about it, probing where we can, and working out what they're up to and why someone thought Simone and Aline had to be killed.'

'The very first time you ask a question of anyone they'll know we didn't buy their version of events,' Macmillan warned him.

'Yes,' said Steven flatly.

Macmillan smiled. 'Have a care,' he said, 'and keep me informed.'

Steven left Macmillan's office and paused to speak to Jean Roberts. He produced a copy of the participant list for the Prague meeting and asked her to check affiliations.

'What am I looking for?'

'Anything that doesn't match up. Check out the stated university connections. Anyone listed as being attached to a university which turns out to have never heard of them I'd like to know about. Anyone with known connections to the intelligence community . . . anyone known to the police . . . and perhaps more important, anyone who looks dodgy to you, Jean.'

Jean smiled, pleased as always to be credited with the capacity to spot pieces that didn't belong in the jigsaw – a talent developed through many years with Sci-Med. She'd been with John Macmillan since its inception. 'Will do. Anything else?'

'I'd like a contact number for a man named Bill Andrews: he's on the list as the man who deals with American charity money.'

Steven was about to leave when Jean reached into her desk drawer and withdrew a folder which she handed to him. 'Sir John thought you might like to look this over at your leisure, just to keep you up to speed with what's going on in the world of ME.'

Steven accepted the file with a small smile but without comment and went to his office. He was wondering what it would be like right now along the north Pakistan border, an area he knew reasonably well, having visited it on more than one occasion in his Special Forces past. He remembered the feeling at the time that he could have been on the moon, so lonely and desolate was the region. It also had a history of being bad news for any country stupid enough to imagine they could control and bring stability to it – not that that had ever stopped them trying.

The current situation there was worse than ever. The legacy of Bush's war on terror had left Afghanistan without any credible government save for a bunch of puppets who were being assassinated on a regular basis by the Taleban, and on the other side of the border the Pakistani government was so corrupt that it made a corkscrew look like a spirit level thanks to an ill-advised release from prison of more than nine thousand crooks in an amnesty in 2007. Against that background, attempting to find out why two young doctors whose only ambition had been to help and protect children had been murdered was not going to be easy, but he would give it his best shot.

His starting hypothesis had to be that Simone and Aline had come across something other than the fact that one of the aid teams on the ground – probably more – were fake. They were American intelligence-gathering units but in imitation of genuine aid teams they had a Pakistani element to them. The CIA man at the meeting he'd just attended had mentioned a Pakistani doctor in the team whose work Simone and Aline had come across and there would probably have been an interpreter too.

According to Aline, the team had come across a village where people were falling ill and children's polio vaccination schedules hadn't been completed. This had alarmed Simone . . . wait. What had? He, like the others, had been assuming that it was the problem with the children's vaccinations that had given her cause for concern, but it could have been the fact that people in the village were ill. What was wrong with them? Had they contracted polio? Simone and Aline would have known if that had been the case, but Aline had just said that people were ill . . . and that she and Simone had taken blood samples!

This could be the break he was looking for. They had taken blood samples for lab analysis but what had they done with them? Where had they sent them? The lab reports might answer a whole lot of questions.

TWELVE

Steven recognised that he was about to ask the first question, the one Macmillan had highlighted as having inevitable repercussions, but he couldn't see any way round it: he had to know where the samples had been sent and what the lab had found. The only thing he had to decide was whom to ask. A moment's thought pointed him at Guy Monfils at *Médecins Sans Frontières* in Paris: he would know exactly where his teams would send lab samples and maybe, as a bonus, he wouldn't have to tell anyone he'd been asked . . .

'Guy? It's Steven Dunbar in London.'

It only took Steven a few moments to conclude that Monfils had swallowed the official line about Aline's involvement with drug traffickers. 'A tremendous shock,' he called it. 'She must have succumbed to temptation, poor girl.' If he believed that, thought Steven, he would almost certainly be happy with Simone's death being recorded as an accident and had probably accepted the CIA's apology for their tactics along with the other major aid agencies. There would be no point in even attempting to recruit Monfils as an ally. It wasn't that he was uncaring or a fool; he was just used to seeing the best in people and placing his trust in authority.

'I have a question, Guy.'

Steven asked about lab facilities for aid workers in the field. 'It must be really difficult?'

'It can be a nightmare, Steven. Even keeping the vaccines cool is a major headache.'

'So what do you do about actual lab work in the field . . . blood grouping, biochemistry, microbiology, that sort of thing?'

'We have technicians out there who perform basic tests, but for major things the teams have to send samples back to Europe.'

'To France?'

'Or London.'

C'mon, c'mon, thought Steven, just a bit more . . .

'The teams working on polio eradication would use Dr North's lab in London. Virology is not something you can do in the field.'

'Of course not,' said Steven, as if he hadn't just received a crucial piece of information when in reality he felt like a lottery winner.

'May I ask why you want to know this?'

Steven had anticipated the question and had given his answer some thought. He said, 'I'm giving a talk to medical students about the practice of medicine under testing conditions. I'm aware, of course, from my own experience how the military go about things, but it struck me that your people must face similar problems every day. I thought I'd check with someone who knew and I'm very much obliged to you. You've been a great help.'

'Don't mention it. I hope it goes well for you . . . Maybe you could point some of your students in our direction? We're always on the lookout for committed young people.'

'I'll certainly mention it.'

Steven wondered for a few moments if he'd got away without arousing suspicion. He thought there was a fair chance he had, but questioning Tom North about blood samples from Afghanistan might turn out to be a whole new ball game – but one that would have to wait until tomorrow. First, he wanted to follow a hunch. He opened his wallet and took out the card the French policeman, Le Grice, had given him when they had discussed the sharing of information. Philippe Le Grice had impressed him as being bright – perhaps too bright to succeed in a profession where kissing the right arses and doing things by the book tended to pave the way to the higher echelons. It would be interesting to hear his take on developments in the Aline Lagarde case.

Le Grice wasn't available when Steven called but he rang back thirty minutes later just as Steven was thinking of leaving for the day.

'So, Aline Lagarde was a big bad drug dealer,' said Steven, not bothering to remove the scepticism from his voice.

'Apparently so.'

'Your people must have come up with some pretty convincing evidence?'

'Not my people,' said Le Grice. 'Apparently our drugs squad have had their eye on her for some time . . . although strangely my friend in Drugs didn't seem to know anything about it.'

'But let me guess, your intelligence people did?'

'They came up with so much information . . . in such a short space of time . . . We are truly blessed to have such talent at our disposal.'

Steven judged the time right to make his appeal. 'Philippe, an experienced detective like you must know that something wasn't quite right?'

'The smell was overpowering.'

'But?'

'Madame Le Grice has plans for my pension.'

'So the case is closed?'

'Oh no, not until Dr Lagarde's killer is brought to justice. The investigation will continue . . . with all the vigour you might expect where a drug dealer and a gangland killing is involved.'

'Her parents will be very pleased,' said Steven flatly.

There was a long pause before Le Grice said, 'Of course, if you should happen to uncover something that contradicts the official version of events . . .'

'I'll let you know.'

'Have a care, Steven. I think you have a saying . . . discretion is the better part of valour?'

'Point taken.'

Steven drove north to Leicester: he was in the flat when Tally got home at ten thirty and gave him a peck on the cheek before plumping herself down beside him.

'Well, honey, how was your day?' Steven mimicked in US sitcom style.

'There aren't enough expletives in the world to describe my day,' Tally replied. 'Do you think these people who go to church on Sundays and prattle on about all things bright and beautiful ever think about the microbial world and what bacteria and viruses do to people?'

'I think the deal is God only gets credit, not blame.'

'Just like the bloody government.'

'Exactly. Only previous governments get blame.'

'I've got an interview at Great Ormond Street.'

'That's wonderful.'

'Let's not count our chickens. It's one of the best children's hospitals in the world, remember. Competition will be fierce.'

'The best should employ the best. You'll walk it.'

'We'll see,' said Tally, getting up. 'How about you? What was the mystery meeting about?'

Steven told her and Tally's eyes opened wide in astonishment. 'Fake aid teams? They were pretending to vaccinate children and leaving them unprotected in a polio endemic area? Is there nothing those bastards won't stoop to? How many kids have they left paralysed so they could bring in the man who shot their "paw"?'

'There's more,' said Steven thoughtfully. 'They're covering up something else, something big enough for MI6, the CIA and possibly French intelligence to be involved in. I'm convinced Simone and Aline were murdered because they stumbled into it.'

Tally's anger was being replaced by alarm. She pursed her lips. 'Steven, I know this is all awful but . . . you can't bring them back . . . and if the Foreign Secretary and MI6 are involved . . . they're on our side, aren't they? Wouldn't you be going up against . . . your own?'

'Sometimes a man's gotta do what a man's gotta do . . .'

'Don't you start! This is not a joking matter. You don't have to do this at all.'

Steven stared at the floor for what Tally thought was an eternity before he looked up and said apologetically, 'I think I do.'

Tally felt a hollow appear in her stomach. She nodded slowly. 'I suppose you do. Drink?'

'Please.'

Steven called Tom North in the morning and asked about the samples Simone and Aline had taken from the sick people in the village they'd come across, resigned to the fact that by lunchtime Whitehall would know about the inquiry.

'I don't think I dealt with them personally, but I can certainly find out for you if it's important?' North replied.

'I'd just like to know why so many people, including children, had fallen ill,' said Steven. 'As I understand it, the fake aid teams the Americans put in would account for the kids not being vaccinated properly against polio . . . but that wouldn't make anyone sick, would it?'

'Certainly not,' agreed North. 'Unless, of course, it was actually an outbreak of polio.'

'Which Simone and Aline would have recognised,' said Steven. 'In which case, there probably would have been no need to send samples for investigation. Maybe that's what Simone wanted to talk to you about when she came to London?'

'Could be. Look, why don't I look into this? Maybe you could pop into the lab and I'll fill you in on what I come up with?'

Steven arranged to meet North at ten the following morning.

THIRTEEN

Edinburgh

'Mummy, can Mark come in to play after school today?' asked seven-year-old David Leeming.

'If his mummy says it's all right,' his mother, Julie, replied.

'Can Sally come in too?' piped up David's younger sister, Joanne.

'No, Sally was here yesterday. It's David's turn to have a friend in. Maybe tomorrow.'

'That's not fair,' complained Joanne, pouting her lower lip.

'Yes, it is,' insisted her brother.

'If you two don't get a move on, you're going to keep Daddy waiting and you know he hates being late. He'll stop your pocket money if he is and serve you right.'

Julie hid a small smile as the bickering stopped and was replaced with slurping sounds as the pair finished their cereal in double quick time.

John Leeming, short, bespectacled and balding, came into the kitchen, a briefcase hanging open from one hand as he stuffed papers into it with the other. 'You guys about ready?'

'They certainly are,' replied Julie, exchanging a knowing smile with her children.

The sound of the letterbox opening and closing interrupted them and Julie said, 'Jo, be a darling and fetch Daddy's paper.'

Joanne disappeared into the hall and was away for longer than expected.

'Jo, what are you doing?'

Julie's question was answered when she looked up to see her five year old standing there with excrement all over her hands and a shocked, puzzled look on her face as she started to sob.

'Oh, Christ, John, they've done it again,' exclaimed Julie as she rushed her daughter off to the downstairs lavatory. 'The bastards . . . the absolute bastards.'

Mark, upset by the goings on and the fact that his mother was behaving so out of character, sat wide-eyed at the table and asked with a quavering voice, 'Why, Daddy? Why did they do that?'

His father, filled with anger and frustration, snapped, 'I don't know, Mark. I really don't.'

Dr John Leeming was fast approaching his wits' end. A research virologist with over twenty years' experience who had been working for the last five years to establish the cause of myalgic encephalomyelitis, couldn't understand why he and his family had become the target in recent months of fanatics who seemed to have decided that the failure of researchers like him and others to find the cause of the condition had been deliberate. This was the second time the 'nutters', as he thought of them, had put excrement through their letterbox. He snatched at the phone, intent on venting his anger at the police and murmuring, 'They'll be up on the bloody ring road booking motorists for being two miles an hour over the limit . . .'

'It's damned well happened again . . .' he began as he got an answer and Julie returned with their cleaned-up daughter.

'This can't go on, John,' she murmured as her husband ended his call and the children, now blazered and carrying their lunch boxes, preceded them out into the hall.

'I know, I know. I'll speak to the prof today. Maybe it's time we reassessed our research priorities.'

As they opened the front door, John noticed an envelope stuck to the outside with Sellotape. He exchanged a look with Julie before unsticking it and gingerly examining the outside for contamination. He tore it open.

IT'S NOT SHIT ON THE FLOOR, IT'S ALL IN YOUR MIND.

'Bastards,' repeated Julie.

Birmingham

Molly Freeman, senior lecturer in microbiology at the University of Birmingham, turned over in bed and stretched out her arm to find an empty space. It was something she wished she could stop doing: it only made her angry and got the day off to a bad start. It had been fully three months since her husband Barry had succumbed to the charms of Marion Philby, one of his PhD students – 'the tart' as Molly knew her – and decided that the grass would be greener without Molly on it any more. He and the tart had set up home in a small flat in Edgbaston while she remained in the family home – a detached villa on a housing estate on the edge of the city – with their ten-year-old son Jamie until such time as they could 'come to an arrangement' as her husband had put it. She knew Barry was hoping for a 'civilised' agreement while her own preferred 'arrange-ment' would involve taking him to the cleaners and nailing him upside down to a tree along with the tart. In fact, she had a meeting planned with her lawyer that afternoon to that end.

'Jamie, are you up yet?' she called out as she slid out of bed and found her wrap.

A sleepy reply of 'Yes' failed to convince and she put her head round her son's bedroom door to say to the recumbent form under the covers, 'If that's up, the laws of physics will have to be rewritten.' She didn't say it unkindly. She was only too aware of how badly Jamie had taken his father's defection.

'Five more minutes . . .' came the groan.

'Three.'

'Deal.'

Later, as they sat having breakfast, Molly tried to maintain light conversation although she did most of the talking while her son would grunt at intervals when pressed.

'I thought we might catch a film this weekend; what d'you think?'

'What's on?'

'I don't know, but we can look in the paper later and decide. Okay?'

'Mmm.'

Do you want a lift or are you taking your bike?'

'Lift please.'

'Right, get a move on. I've got a research group meeting at nine.'

Molly held the door for her son as he combined putting on his school rucksack with stuffing a last piece of toast into his mouth. 'You didn't clean your shoes last night,' she observed as he passed her, before something more important struck them both.

'The tyres are flat,' said Jamie.

'More than flat,' said his mother, walking up to her Renault Clio in the drive and seeing that they'd been slashed. A message had been scratched into the bonnet. THE TYRES ARE NOT FLAT. IT'S ALL IN YOUR MIND.

'Oh Christ,' murmured Julie.

'What does it mean, Mum? Did Dad do that?'

'No, Jamie,' said Julie quickly, alarmed that what had passed between Barry and herself could have put such an idea into his head. 'Someone doesn't like my research very much.'

'I'm scared, Mum.'

Julie put her arm round his shoulders. 'I'm not too chipper myself,' she murmured. 'Maybe it's time for a change . . .'

London

Professor Maurice Langley, head of research at the Medical Research Council's Investigative Microbiology Unit at Hammersmith Hospital, decided his day was done and packed a few papers into his briefcase before putting on his coat and heading for the exit. He said good night to the man on the door – an ex-soldier who always straightened himself to his full height before replying – and crossed the car park to where his new black BMW 5 series sat, front wheels turned at a jaunty angle as if impatient to be driven off into the night by a man who went his own way.

It gave him pleasure to see it there. Like many academics he'd been used to driving a series of second-hand bangers throughout his career – something that went with the image of being too cerebral to care about material things – but at the age of fifty he and his wife had decided that a successful man deserved a bit of respect from Joe Public and the new Beemer fitted the bill perfectly.

Langley got in and sat for a moment enjoying the feeling of being cocooned in a world of silence and leather. He turned on Mozart who had been patiently waiting in the CD player and prepared to set off for home. The only thing to spoil the moment was the knife in the gloved hand that reached over from the back seat. It now nestled against his throat, cold and very threatening.

'Take a left and drive till I tell you different.'

Langley's pulse rate was pushing two hundred and he had to fight to control his bladder and bowels. 'What d'you want?' he stammered. 'Is it the car? Look, you can have it; just don't hurt me. Let me go . . .'

'The car?' snorted the voice in the back. 'Is this what you deserve for being fuck all use, you wanker? Just drive.'

After twenty minutes, Langley was instructed to pull over and stop. They were passing through a deserted area with woodland on both sides. Seeing woodland brought up images of decomposing bodies in shallow graves for Langley. He thought the worst. 'Oh my God, no,' he pleaded, his voice going up an octave.

'Shut up and move across to the passenger seat.'

Langley did as he was told, his collar being held firmly.

'Put your hands behind your head.'

Langley felt his wrists being tied to the head restraint pillars. He was then blindfolded and could only listen as his assailant got out and into the driving seat. He was aware of the car turning round and heading back into the city. 'Where are you taking me?'

His question remained unanswered and he sat in terrified silence for another ten minutes until he heard the wheels of the car crunch on gravel and they came to a halt. He was untied and told to get out. The blindfold stayed on.

'You got him then?' asked a new voice.

'Piece of cake. Got the jag ready?'

'And the suit,' came the reply.

Confusion was added to the terror Langley was in. What was that about a Jag? Why were they putting him in a Jaguar? It was only when he felt the sharp needle stab in his buttock that he realised he'd got the meaning of 'jag' all wrong. The lights went out.

When Langley came to he was no longer blindfolded and he could move freely. The problem was, he couldn't see properly. There were bright lights everywhere but he couldn't focus on anything. He was in a world of rainbow-coloured blurs. There was noise – lots of it: traffic noise and people laughing. He searched for his phone in his pocket but found he had no pockets. These weren't his clothes. He was wearing some strange kind of outfit or costume.

The people in Leicester Square could see it was a clown costume and it was being worn by a man who was staggering around with a message taped to his back. It said, I'M LOOKING FOR THE CAUSE OF ME.

People were laughing, assuming that it must be part of some stag-night prank . . . although the age of the clown and his apparent distress perhaps suggested not . . . but, of course, it was better not to get involved. That was the British way. They body-swerved past the clown on their way to their nights out.

Langley was totally disorientated. The swirling bright lights and the feeling of nausea prevented him from making any meaningful contact with the vague figures that flitted in and out of his distorted vision. He reached out and touched someone who smacked his hand away.

'What's your game then?'

Langley recoiled from the angry voice and changed direction, only to feel himself stumble as he unwittingly stepped off the pavement . . . unfortunately, into the path of a bus. The sound of the horn, the screech of brakes, the thud of the impact as the front of the bus hit Langley and the cries of bus passengers thrown from their seats all blended into some hellish cacophony before fading to nothing as stunned onlookers froze and looked down at the broken body of a very dead clown.

FOURTEEN

Steven arrived at City College just before ten and, as before, was asked to wait until someone from the North group came down to escort him to the lab. It was the Irish PhD student he'd met last time, Liam Kelly.

'I'm afraid Tom's not in yet,' said Liam. 'Most unlike him, but he shouldn't be long. Must have been held up in traffic.'

Steven was shown into North's office and invited to sit. Liam handed him the current copy of *Nature*. 'Maybe you'd like to have a look while you wait?'

Steven thanked him and started to flick through the magazine. Ten minutes later, as he was reading about the continuing search for the Higgs boson particle, he heard a female voice out in the lab say, 'Liam, Tom's car's in the car park.'

Steven looked up to see Liam Kelly join the girl he remembered as Jenny Davis, the student who was working on herpes simplex. They were both looking out the window.

'Stupid – it's just dawned on me. It's been there for a while. He must be in the building somewhere.'

'It's not like him to forget he had a meeting,' said Kelly. 'I'll get them to page him.'

Another five minutes went by with still no sign of North. Liam apologised profusely to Steven and said he would go look for his supervisor. In the meantime, Steven chatted to Jenny about her work but stopped in mid-sentence when, over her shoulder, he saw Liam Kelly down in the car park cross over to North's car and look in the window. The hairs on the back of his neck stood up when he saw Liam recoil at something he'd discovered. The boy turned away from the car and threw up on the ground before supporting himself on a neighbouring car with both hands.

'Something's wrong,' Steven blurted out to Jenny, who had her back to the window. He rushed out of the lab and ran down the stairs rather than wait for a lift. Ignoring Liam's predicament, he ran straight to North's car and looked in the driver's window to see North slumped over the wheel. It was clear he had been shot through the back of the head.

There was no possibility of his still being alive so Steven did not disturb the body. North was facing away from him with his right cheek on the steering wheel so he walked round to the other side of the car and saw the dead face of Tom North with the bullet's exit wound in the middle of his forehead. Something else caught his attention and caused him to shudder. Half the index finger on North's left hand had been cut off: it was lying on the floor of the car. He'd been tortured before he'd been shot. Steven called the police and remained by the car until they arrived, making sure that no one interfered with the scene of the crime.

Liam had now been joined by the others from the lab, Dan Hausman, Jenny and two of the technicians, as well as people from elsewhere in the building. Steven ushered the curious away from the car, leaving it to Liam to tell them what had happened. The police arrived within minutes, led by an inspector from the Metropolitan Police who barked instructions to his officers.

After the initial hustle and bustle and taping-off of the crime scene, Steven was surprised to see them suddenly resort to doing virtually nothing. He showed the inspector his ID and asked what the problem was.

'I've been instructed to wait.'

'For what?'

'Good question.'

The question was answered minutes later when a chief super-intendent from Special Branch arrived accompanied by another man in plain clothes who didn't introduce himself. He didn't need to as far as Steven was concerned: he knew him. It was John Ricksen, an MI5 officer.

Ricksen did a double take when he saw Steven and came over. The two men shook hands but felt uneasy about each other's presence. They had crossed paths before on assignment, and although not friends had a civilised relationship and had done each other small favours in the past. MI5 didn't care much for Sci-Med, seeing them as a loose cannon, while Sci-Med people tended to believe that MI5 weren't overly blessed with imagination.

'What brings you to City College?' Ricksen asked.

'I had an appointment to speak to the deceased.'

'Not much chance of that now. Dare I ask what about?'

'Polio in Afghanistan.'

'Right . . .' replied Ricksen slowly, as if wondering if this were a wind-up. 'Not exactly Sci-Med territory.'

Knowing that his presence here and his continuing interest in the situation in Pakistan and Afghanistan would be all over Whitehall in a couple of hours, Steven said, 'North was collaborating with a friend of mine, Simone Ricard. She died in an "accident". Looks like North had one too.'

'Hardly an accident . . . Oh, I see. You don't think that . . .'

Steven shrugged. 'Well, I've told you what I'm doing here. What's your interest?

'North was on our list.'

'Of what?'

'Possible terrorist targets.'

Steven raised a questioning eyebrow.

'I take it you know about the fake aid teams the Yanks used in their hunt for Bin Laden?'

Steven nodded. 'I know.'

'It caused quite a lot of bad feeling in the region. The extremists saw their chance to tar everyone with the same brush and have been doing their best to have everyone believe that the genuine polio eradication people were complicit in the whole sorry business.'

'Were they?'

'Good God, no. It was purely a CIA operation. Looks like North has just become collateral damage, as our colleagues across the pond are wont to call it.'

Steven said, 'Look at his left hand.'

Ricksen did so and returned with a frown on his face. 'Not quite straightforward revenge then. Someone wanted something from the good doctor. I wonder what.'

As they waited for the medical examiner to attend they were joined by the Special Branch man, who'd been in conversation with the Met inspector. Ricksen introduced him to Steven and drew his attention to what was lying on the floor of the car.

The Special Branch man picked up the severed finger with tweezers he took from his inside pocket and examined it from several angles before dropping it into a plastic bag and saying, 'Well, bang goes the obvious explanation, and it probably wasn't a terrorist attack either. They prefer blowing things to kingdom come: a single shot just ain't their style. That just leaves us the little matter of figuring out who did it and why . . . starting with no bloody idea.'

Steven sought out Liam Kelly, who was sitting with some colleagues, still clearly upset as was Jenny, who dabbed at her eyes with a scrunched-up tissue. 'Could I have a word?' Steven asked softly.

Liam detached himself and Steven said, 'I'm sorry, this is obviously not the time, but I need to speak to someone about blood samples sent to Tom's lab from one of the polio teams in Afghanistan.'

'Dan's your man,' said Liam. 'We all do bits and pieces when required, but Dan is in charge of who does what unless there's some specific problem and then Tom decides . . . decided what happens to them.'

'I can't see Dan around at the moment,' said Steven. 'Maybe you could tell him when you see him that I'll call by the lab tomorrow morning about eleven?'

'Of course.'

Steven called Tally to tell her about Tom North's murder and say that he would be staying at the London flat for the time being, but the call went straight to voicemail, restricting him to minimum detail. He then called John Macmillan to say he was on his way to the Home Office.

'What kind of a mood is he in?' he asked Jean Roberts when he arrived.

'Foul. I'd wear a flak jacket if I were you,' she replied.

Steven raised his eyes heavenwards as the intercom sparked into life. 'Is he here yet?'

'Yes, Sir John, just arrived. I'll send him in.'

Macmillan didn't turn to acknowledge Steven's entry. Instead, he continued to stare at the window across the room, drumming his fingers rapidly but lightly on his desk. Steven stood in silence until a slight turn of the head and a nod indicated that he should sit.

'I've just had the Foreign Secretary on the phone.'

'Really? Is he well?'

Macmillan's look would have curdled milk. 'This is not the time, Steven. I'm not in the mood.'

Steven believed him.

'He was spitting tacks. He thought we'd accepted that Dr Ricard's death was an accident but now he knows differently. He insists that your continued poking around is only going to result in an increasing press interest in what went on before Bin Laden was found and that is really going to piss off our American cousins. He's asked me to rein you in.'

'And you said?'

'I told him that doubts over Dr Ricard's death were yours and yours alone, not the basis of an official Sci-Med investigation. If I were to order you to desist, you'd probably resign and continue anyway.'

Steven's silence confirmed it.

'The Foreign Secretary pointed out that, as employees of HMG, we should be paying more attention to things at home rather than interfering in things that don't concern us, in particular the activities of ME protesters whose actions have now claimed a life with the murder of Professor Langley. I could hardly argue. It's an escalating situation and it's getting out of hand.'

'Well, yes,' Steven conceded reluctantly, 'but murder investigation is a police matter, not something for Sci-Med. There again . . .'

He paused, and Macmillan prompted him to continue.

'There's something not quite right about the whole thing. I had a look through the file . . . I can understand the ME people and their families getting upset about being dismissed as a bunch of neurotics who need psychiatric help. I can understand their frustration translating into paint daubing and tyre slashing – minor acts of vandalism – but pushing people under buses? That just doesn't ring true. I smell a rat.'

Macmillan sighed but nodded his agreement. 'I thought so too. I've been asking around about the chap knocked down by the bus. He wasn't pushed under the wheels as the tabloids suggested; it was an accident. The post-mortem showed that he'd been drugged; he wouldn't have been able to see properly or think clearly. I think it fair to assume that his captors deposited him in a crowded London area to draw attention to their cause. They didn't anticipate his stumbling into the path of a bus. The gutter press, however, saw their chance to whip up a storm of bad feeling.'

'Now that makes much more sense,' Steven agreed. 'It strikes me that Tom North's death, however, is very much something that Sci-Med should be concerned with. He knew or possessed something that someone prepared to use a knife and a gun wanted badly. Maybe we should be concerning ourselves with finding out what that was?'

Macmillan took a deep breath and exhaled slowly before saying, 'I wish I could argue but you do have a point.'

'Both Special Branch and Five turned up at the scene,' Steven continued. 'The official line was that North was a potential target because of his connection with the polio eradication initiative. The Taleban were pretty pissed off with what the CIA did and were prepared to have a go at all aid workers. I'm not sure I buy that.'

FIFTEEN

It was after ten when Steven finally managed to reach Tally. He phoned from his favourite chair by the window in his flat, watching the lights of the river traffic pass by through the gap between buildings across the street to the accompaniment of the dialling tone. He cheered up when she answered.

'Busy girl?'

'Don't go there,' Tally replied. 'That was terrible news about Tom North. What are the police saying?'

'They don't know where to start.' He told her about the torture angle.

'How absolutely awful . . . but maybe that will narrow things down a bit when it comes to motive?'

'Only if you knew what it was the killer was after.'

'I take it that means you've no idea either?' asked Tally.

'None at all, but I suggested to John that it's something Sci-Med should be involved in.'

'Did he agree?'

'I think he does in principle but he's been under increasing pressure to stop me meddling in things that don't concern me and have me investigate the ME problem, which HMG see as a domestic problem that warrants Sci-Med's immediate attention.'

'Good,' said Tally. 'I couldn't agree more.'

'Tally . . .'

'I'm sorry, Steven, but, as I've said before, you can't bring Simone back and the opposition to your involvement is scaring me every time I think about it. You should let sleeping dogs lie.'

'I still feel the ME thing is a matter for the police not us, but HMG are building it up and jumping on the tabloid bandwagon, saying that the protesters are now resorting to murder when they must know full well that that isn't true. Professor Langley's death was a tragic accident. I know that won't be of any comfort to his family but it's nevertheless true.'

'Hmm,' said Tally.

'Having said that, you may well get your way. I don't think John can see a way out of getting Sci-Med involved now that the tabloids are setting the agenda. I may well end up looking for tyre slashers and paint daubers instead of hunting down Simone's killer.'

'Steven . . . I didn't mean . . . I mean, I just worry about you.'

'Tally?'

'What?'

'I love you.'

Steven heard Tally give a slight sigh and the phone went dead. He looked at it, feeling uncomfortable that he hadn't been totally honest with her. He'd given the impression that he was about to give up the search for Simone's killer when that wasn't true. He'd said that he had no idea why Tom North had been murdered when he was actually considering that there might well be a connection between North's death and those of Simone and Aline Lagarde. That was something he hadn't even mentioned to Macmillan. He poured himself a beer, put a Stan Getz album on the stereo, switched out the lights and sat back down in his chair to see if he could spot any stars through the city's light pollution.

Next day, Steven found the members of Tom North's research group sitting together in the main lab on a circle of stools and chairs. They were discussing future prospects – or rather lack of them from the worries he overheard being expressed. He apologised for interrupting and sympathised over the position they found themselves in. 'Must be a worrying time for you guys. I take it you'll be having meetings with the powers that be?'

'Starting this afternoon,' Liam Kelly confirmed. He didn't sound optimistic. 'One at a time when the police have finished with us.'

'You're obviously all highly skilled at what you do.'

'It's grant money that determines employment, not skill,' volunteered one of the technicians. 'The grants all died with Tom.'

'I understand you have some questions about the lab work we do for the Med Sans aid teams in Pakistan and Afghanistan,' said Dan Hausman, changing the subject.

'If that's convenient?'

'Sure,' replied Hausman. He turned to the others. 'Why don't you lot go get some coffee while I talk to Dr Dunbar?' He waited while the others trooped out of the lab, then said, 'So, what would you like to know?'

'I'd like to know how the teams send samples from the field, what sort of things they ask for, what sort of tests you carry out,' replied Steven.

'We only get blood samples,' said Hausman. He got up from his chair and walked over to a tall refrigerator to bring out a wire rack containing several plastic tubes with blood in them. 'Like these. We supply the tubes, which contain a range of chemicals and anticoagulants which are used according to the tests being requested, and they're transported back to us in cool boxes. I have to stress that we don't perform routine tests – they're done on site – we carry out checks related to the polio vaccines the teams are using. Some are experimental so they have to know whether the kids are developing antibodies or not. Straightforward serology really.'

'How about kids who might be developing polio?' asked Steven.

'The diagnosis would probably be made on clinical grounds, but we would be able to confirm it if required.'

'Would you isolate the virus?'

Hausman shook his head. 'Definitely not. We have the capacity to do that but growing high-risk pathogens in the lab is something to be avoided if at all possible. Clinical diagnosis backed up by serology is usually enough.'

'Remind me; why did you guys end up providing this service?'

'Routine virology labs in the UK are not used to dealing with polio; we are. Although we're a research lab, Tom thought it was the least we could do and we're not called upon that often. Call it a PR exercise if you like.'

'The age of the image,' said Steven with a smile.

'Everyone needs one,' agreed Hausman. 'To paraphrase Mr Shakespeare, very little that glisters is gold these days.'

Both men were laughing as the others started to return from their coffee break. 'When was the last time you were called upon to do some tests?' Steven asked.

Hausman looked thoughtful. 'From the North West Frontier? Oh, I dunno, maybe three or four months ago. One of the teams asked us to check the antibody levels in some village kids they weren't sure about.'

'Nothing after that?' asked Steven.

'Don't think so.'

'Some bloods came in from Dr Ricard, Dan,' a voice put in. Liam Kelly had overheard the conversation from the other side of an island bench, where a tall gantry containing bottles of chemicals shielded him from view.

For a moment it appeared to Steven that Hausman didn't quite know which facial expression to adopt. Then he grinned. 'Oh yeah,' he agreed. 'I forgot. Simone sent some bloods for analysis but we didn't carry out the tests. She'd come across some sick village folk. Tom passed them on to another lab.'

'Why was that?'

'We don't do general diagnostic work. She didn't know what was wrong with the people, so it was better that the tests were carried out by a hospital or Public Health lab.'

'Do you happen to know if they found anything?'

'No. I wouldn't see the report, but I believe Tom said not – that's probably why I forgot about it. That's often the way with viruses. Labs often have to leave the diagnosis as a "viral infection" without being specific. GPs tell patients every day that they're suffering from a virus without saying which one. They're just guessing. It's just too damned difficult to establish.'

'I see,' said Steven. 'Which lab was this?'

'I'm not sure . . . maybe Tom made the arrangements. It was probably the Public Health lab at Mill Hill. Is it important?'

'Not really,' said Steven with a smile. 'Many thanks for your help. I hope things work out for you guys.'

'I'll see you out,' said Liam Kelly.

'No need,' Steven replied, before realising that it was probably department policy to see visitors off the premises. He didn't protest again and Liam came down with him in the lift. Steven thought he seemed more circumspect than usual but put it down to worry about whether or not he would be able to continue with his studies. 'I hope they can fix you up with a new supervisor, Liam,' he said as the doors opened.

'Thanks, Dr Dunbar . . . Look, this is probably not important, but . . .'

'Go on.'

'It wasn't Tom who sent off Dr Ricard's blood samples, it was Dan: he must have forgotten.'

'Oh, okay.'

'I saw the package. He sent them to a Dr Neville Henson.'

Steven smiled. 'Thanks for clearing that up, Liam. Good luck this afternoon.'

He kept up the pretence of taking on board an unimportant detail till he got into his car and put his head back on the restraint. 'Sweet Jesus Christ,' he whispered. 'What the fuck is going on?' Alarm bells had gone off in his head as soon as he'd heard the name Henson. Dr Neville Henson didn't work for Public Health at Mill Hill; he worked at Porton Down, the UK's germ warfare establishment or whatever they called it these days. It had been a while since Steven had checked. It was probably the institute for cuddly toys and happy songs by now. Neville Henson was the microbiologist whose name and affiliation had appeared in the list of participants at the Prague polio meeting.

SIXTEEN

Steven was glad that the demands of London traffic stopped him dwelling on what he'd discovered until he reached the sanctuary of the underground car park at Marlborough Court. By this time his anger and frustration had subsided enough to enable him to sit for a couple of minutes with only the contracting metal sounds from the Porsche for company until he had recovered his powers of cold, calm appraisal.

The fact that the blood samples had been sent to Porton would mean a sudden end to that line of inquiry. Porton was a top secret establishment: there would be no point in asking even if he hadn't already been warned off. But the mere fact they'd been sent there said a lot. Blood samples for diagnostic tests would not be sent to Porton unless there was a very good reason, a reason that implied a connection with high risk pathogens or biological weaponry. Polio was a high risk virus but Simone and her team were used to seeing and dealing with it. There would have been no need for Porton to become involved – but they were.

Dr Neville Henson had been present at the meeting in Prague, as had . . . the name wouldn't come to him. Steven got out, locked the car and took the lift upstairs. He switched on the kettle and looked through his paperwork for the list of participants at Prague. Dr Mel Reznik from the Centers for Disease Control and Prevention in Atlanta, Georgia was the name he was looking for. Two scientists from labs dedicated to the study of the world's killer diseases and how they might be developed or altered for military purposes. The CIA's admission of guilt over using fake aid teams in order to gain intelligence clearly wasn't the full story.

Steven had the feeling he was opening Pandora's box. When he thought about it, the confession could even have been a clever ploy to stop further investigation. *Médecins Sans Frontières*, the World Health Organisation and even the UK and French governments all saw the sense in keeping what had happened under wraps. They thought they were defending the polio eradication initiative from prurient press interest and scandal by keeping quiet about what the CIA had done when, in fact, they were unwittingly helping to cover something up. Something else was going on in the border region between Pakistan and Afghanistan, something that had got Simone Ricard, Aline Lagarde and maybe even Tom North killed.

The murder of Tom North was a difficult one. A terrorist assassination couldn't be ruled out entirely if, as Ricksen had said, North had been on their at-risk register, although the torture aspect made it more problematical and the manner of his killing was, as the Special Branch man had said, out of character. Explosives rather than knives were usually the choice of Islamic terrorists when it came to achieving their ends. But if North's death was linked to what Simone had stumbled across, it suggested that North might not have been part of it, whereas his senior post-doc's faulty recollection of when blood samples from Simone had been received and what had happened to them put him very firmly on the naughty step. Steven needed to know a lot more about Daniel Hausman.

He turned on his laptop and found an encrypted message that had come in from Jean Roberts. She had obtained contact details for Bill Andrews, the charity money administrator who had been with Simone in the gallery at the Strahov monastery library. He and the organisation he worked for were based in Kansas City – a long way from Wall Street, thought Steven. Mind you, so was charity. He checked his watch: the time difference suggested he give it another hour or so.

Jean had also included her report on the participants at the Prague meeting. Her conclusions were that everyone was who they said they were but some had 'more interesting' backgrounds than others. She had listed those on a separate sheet: Dan Hausman was among them. Hausman had obtained his PhD from UCLA – the University of California at Los Angeles – before being recruited by the military and posted to Fort Detrick, the US equivalent of Porton Down. His PhD thesis had been on virus–cell interactions. As expected, there was no indication of what he had worked on at Fort Detrick. He had then left the military and sponsorship by the US pharmaceutical company Reeman Losch had enabled his secondment as a post-doctoral fellow to Tom North's lab in London. Jean had added a note saying that Reeman Losch were not big players in pharmaceuticals – they weren't quoted on the New York stock exchange – and that their special interest was in anti-viral compounds. It wasn't clear where their income came from as only one of their products – an anti-retro-viral agent – had come on the market. Since they were a private company, there was no way of scrutinising their accounts. Try US intelligence, thought Steven. To his way of thinking it seemed probable that Reeman Losch was a front for them, given Hausman's time at Fort Detrick and then his sponsored fellowship in the North lab.

The picture was building. Reznik from CDC Atlanta, Henson from Porton Down and Hausman from Fort Detrick all had an interest in the Prague meeting and what was going on in the border region between Pakistan and Afghanistan.

Bill Andrews also appeared on Jean's list of 'interesting' people. A graduate of Harvard Business School, he had worked briefly for an investment bank in New York before being recruited into the CIA. His career remained a blank until he surfaced again, this time working in financial management for the charity Children First before moving to his current position with the body that oversaw all American charitable contributions to health in the third world.

'Well, well, well,' murmured Steven. 'Enter the CIA.' He sat back in his chair and let out a long sigh. It was odds on that Andrews still worked for the CIA, and his connection with Children First could hardly be coincidence. It was almost certainly he who set up the false aid teams under the umbrella of Children First. Now, as financial controller of all charitable monies collected in the US for health projects in far-away places, he was in a position to direct funds to wherever the CIA wanted them to go. In fact, the CIA could actually fund their own projects under the guise of charitable contributions.

Jean had added a codicil pointing out that another participant at the Prague meeting, Dr Ranjit Khan, had been a classmate of Andrews at Harvard: they had shared an apartment. Khan had returned to his native Pakistan after graduating and was believed to be working for Pakistani intelligence – currently a somewhat fractured body thought to be at odds with the present government. It was possible that he had been responsible for supplying the Pakistani element in the fake aid teams.

Steven stared at this last piece of information with the feeling that he was missing something. He prided himself on not missing much. Paying attention to detail was an important part of his job. Even if it didn't appear significant at the time, a small detail could later prove to be the missing part in a puzzle – or even save a life. He remembered what it was. When he'd asked Bill Andrews about who had been present in the gallery when Simone had fallen, Andrews had mentioned Khan, saying, 'The Pakistani doctor who was with us – Dr Khan, I think his name was,' as if he hadn't known him.

Steven got up and walked over to the window to look out at the rain. Andrews and Khan both worked for intelligence services, had probably collaborated over the setting up of fake aid teams and had been with Simone at the time of her fall. They then came down from the gallery and put on a Greek tragedy for the benefit of onlookers with much weeping and wailing. They didn't know it yet but by Christ they were going to pay for it . . . in spades.

Steven turned his thoughts to Aline Lagarde and who might have killed her. Andrews? Khan? Khan hadn't been at Simone's funeral: he'd had to return to Pakistan, according to . . . Andrews. Was that the truth or could Andrews have been covering for Aline's killer? Steven had been planning to phone Andrews to quiz him about who had lost a contact lens in the gallery on that fateful day, but things had moved on apace. He was now almost sure that Andrews and Khan had cooperated in Simone's murder. He called Inspector Philippe Le Grice in Paris instead.

After an exchange of pleasantries Steven came directly to the point. 'I have a favour to ask.'

'In connection with the death of Aline Lagarde?'

'Yes. I think it possible she was murdered by a Pakistani intelligence officer named Dr Ranjit Khan. His cover is that of an aid worker in the villages of the Pakistani/Afghan border. The official story is that he attended the conference in Prague where Simone Ricard died and then returned directly to Pakistan. I think he may have come to France. Is there any way you can check immigration records for the relevant dates?'

'Normally, yes,' replied Le Grice, sounding unsure. 'But given the involvement of our intelligence services in the investigation into Dr Lagarde's death, they might wonder why I want to know.'

'I take your point,' said Steven. 'But there's a good chance they know nothing about Khan. I don't think even they know the whole story.'

'But they came up with the evidence against Dr Lagarde.'

'I think they were involved in trashing her reputation but I don't think they knew anything about the killing. They were acting under orders to keep a CIA operation in Afghanistan out of the limelight.'

'I thought *you* guys were the Americans' poodles,' said Le Grice.

'I've got a sore paw.'

'I'll see what I can do.'

Steven felt guilty about asking Le Grice to do something that might rebound badly on the detective if he were wrong and French intelligence did know more than he thought they did. The phone interrupted his train of thought. It was Jean Roberts.

'Hello, Steven. John was wondering if you had any more thoughts to offer on the ME problem? I think the Home Secretary has been inquiring.'

Steven's feelings of guilt shifted direction. He hadn't actually got round to re-examining the file Jean had given him in detail. He should have remembered that although he and John knew that Langley's death had been an unplanned accident, that was not the official line and the police had probably been encouraged to think differently.

'I haven't reached any conclusions as yet,' he replied. 'But I'm working on it.'

'Then that's what I'll tell him,' said Jean, giving Steven the awful feeling that she could read his mind. 'I'll let him know you'll be in touch soon.'

Steven interpreted the word 'soon' as 'get a move on'. 'Thanks, Jean.'

He found it hard to switch his attention from the progress he had been making on an international platform to events at home involving threatening letters, paint daubing and the letting down of tyres, but he opened the file and started reading.

SEVENTEEN

After an hour, Steven's initial feeling that he was looking at trivial crimes which had nothing to do with Sci-Med started to falter as he picked up on a puzzling feature about the ME affair. He paused to make more coffee and was cursing the fact that his Gaggia espresso maker was leaking all over the place when the phone rang. He thought it might be Philippe Le Grice, but it was Tally.

'Good news. I've got an evening off. Can you come up?'

Another guilt attack. 'Tally, I can't. I've got to get a report ready by tomorrow morning.'

'What a pity.'

'I'm already way behind.'

'Ah me, then my disappointment will probably lead to the appearance of the wicked witch of the west on the wards tomorrow. Think of the children, Steven, think of the poor children . . .'

Steven couldn't help smiling as he started to waver.

'You could always work on your report . . . afterwards?'

'I'm on my way. Book us in for dinner somewhere nice.'

Steven found himself sitting at Tally's kitchen table at two in the morning, wearing T-shirt and boxer shorts, working on his report for Macmillan. The one saving grace was that he did feel perfectly relaxed. Tally was sleeping soundly.

The same feeling of puzzlement he'd felt earlier reappeared as he moved through the file making occasional notes about time and place. Ostensibly, the ME protesters, whoever they were, were objecting to government money being put into psychiatric evaluation instead of what they regarded as proper research – a hunt for the virus causing the condition . . . so why on earth were they targeting the very people who were carrying out the sort of research they wanted? Why weren't they attacking the psychiatrists and psychologists who were getting the grant money? Why weren't they labelling *their* efforts as pointless and a waste of time? And who were the people carrying out the attacks? They didn't seem to have any official voice. Anyone from the ME groups willing to be interviewed seemed to deplore what they saw as crude publicity stunts. The perpetrators always seemed to be people unknown to the official bodies.

The explanation given by them for attacking microbiologists – almost exclusively appearing in the form of graffiti because no one was ever willing to justify their actions in person – was that the scientists weren't doing their job properly: they couldn't be if they hadn't found the virus; they must be deliberately delaying to keep themselves in a job. There seemed to be no appreciation of the fact that if the protesters kept harassing and attacking these people, perhaps forcing them to change fields, there would be no one left looking for a biological cause at all.

Steven shook his head in bemusement. 'Why, why, why?' he murmured.

'Delilah,' whispered a sleepy voice behind him. Tally put her arms round him. 'God, I feel so guilty. You're working through the night and all because of my need for your gorgeous body . . .'

'Understandable,' murmured Steven.

'Bastard.'

'Ah, the fickleness of women . . .'

'How's your report going?'

'I've got enough to make Sir John believe I've been working my bottom off . . . which gives me an idea . . .' said Steven, getting up and turning to enfold Tally, his hands placed firmly on her buttocks.

'No, no,' she giggled. 'The report . . . the report . . .'

*   *   *

114

John Macmillan sat at his desk, massaging his temples as he thought about what Steven had said. 'God, nothing is ever straightforward, is it?' he complained. 'Let me get this straight. You seem to be suggesting that someone other than the ME sufferers might be behind the attacks on researchers because they want to stop research being carried out on it?'

'I'm just saying it's a possibility,' said Steven. 'Otherwise the attacks don't make sense. Why scare people out of doing what you want them to do in the first place?'

'Mmm.'

Steven had to stifle a yawn behind his hand.

'Am I boring you?' snapped Macmillan. He didn't miss much.

'Sorry. Insomnia . . . lot on my mind.'

'As I recall, you were going to the North lab yesterday?'

Steven took a deep breath. 'Yes, and I'm glad I did. I'm pretty sure I know who killed Simone, and possibly Aline as well.'

Macmillan turned round, his eyes wide. 'You know?'

'Mainly thanks to Jean's work in getting me background info on the people attending the Prague meeting. I think Simone's death was caused by two of the official participants, one an American aid administrator named Bill Andrews who's almost certainly CIA, and a Pakistani doctor named Ranjit Khan. He's almost certainly Pakistani intelligence.'

Steven went on to fill in the details leading to his conclusion, ending with, 'I'm waiting to hear back from Inspector Le Grice about Khan's movements.'

Macmillan had returned to his desk. 'Do you have any thoughts on why they did it?'

Steven shook his head. 'I'm convinced there's some kind of two-tier cover-up going on. Some of the big players – maybe even our own government – believe they're conspiring with the Americans to keep the use of fake teams by the CIA hunting for Bin Laden a secret. It's not that they approve of it: they simply don't want to damage the polio eradication initiative beyond repair. But that's not all they're doing. They're unwittingly helping to cover up something else.'

'Which is?'

'I don't know.'

Macmillan looked thoughtful, almost trance-like, as he considered what Steven had told him. It was a look Steven recognised and respected: he waited patiently for the outcome.

'Difficult,' began Macmillan. 'We're short of friends. The involvement of MI6, the CIA, Pakistani intelligence and God knows who else means that we can't look for help in either working out what's going on or in seeking justice for your friend. The only vulnerable point would appear to be Dr Hausman. Before Jean's painstaking work there was a chance that he might just have sent the samples on to Porton because he'd been told to, but in the light of Jean's findings about him and the supposed pharmaceutical company sponsoring him that must be deemed unlikely. He must know what's going on.'

Steven couldn't fault Macmillan's logic. 'Unfortunately, we don't have a pretext for arresting or even questioning him. He's done nothing wrong.'

Macmillan went into thoughtful mode again before coming up with, 'If what you say is true about there being a two-tier cover-up . . . perhaps we could jolt the well-meaning cover-uppers into asking some embarrassing questions of their colleagues.'

'What do you have in mind?'

'Exposing Dr Hausman's Fort Detrick background and CIA connections along with the questionable credentials of his sponsor pharmaceutical company, Reeman Losch. People might then start to wonder what else the CIA have been up to.'

'Divide and conquer.'

'I can't see us doing much conquering,' countered Macmillan. 'But a bit of a rift might be a start.'

'How will you do it?'

Macmillan glanced at his watch. 'I'm having lunch with the director of MI5 today. I'll ask openly about Hausman and Reeman Losch. No doubt he'll . . . mention our interest.'

'Light blue touch paper and retire immediately,' said Steven, remembering the old firework warning.

'In the meantime,' said Macmillan, looking thoughtful, 'I'm going to take you off the ME thing and pass it over to one of your colleagues. If what you've worked out about this two-tier cover-up business proves correct, you've got enough on your plate. All right with you?'

'Absolutely. Who's the lucky boy?'

'I think I'll give it to Scott Jamieson. He's done a good job in uncovering the hospital supplies scam up in Manchester. It's time to hand that one over to the police. He'll welcome a new challenge.'

'He's a good bloke,' said Steven.

'All right to brief him with your thoughts on the subject?'

'Of course.'

Steven returned to his office, pausing to thank Jean Roberts for the excellent work she'd done on screening the people at the Prague meeting.

'You look tired,' she said. 'Can I get you some coffee?'

Steven was sipping his coffee and thinking about Tally when his phone went. It was Philippe Le Grice in Paris.

'I have some news for you.'

'Anything interesting?'

'Very. You were right in your suspicions. Dr Khan did not return to Pakistan immediately after the Prague meeting. He was a passenger on board a flight from Prague to Paris the day before Simone Ricard's funeral.'

'So he *was* in Paris when Aline was killed?'

'There's no doubt about it. He left France the morning after Aline Lagarde's murder.'

'He's your man, Philippe.'

'Thank you, Steven. I only hope we can prove it and restore Dr Lagarde's reputation, but I suspect it won't be that easy. A DNA match might do it, but as you might expect from a hotel room, we have DNA profiles for a number of unidentified individuals. I just hope we get the chance to compare them with Khan's.'

'It might be a good idea to make sure the samples you have are kept in a secure place, considering third party involvement in the case,' suggested Steven.

'Quite so.'

Steven thanked Le Grice for his valuable help. Now that he had proof that Andrews had been lying about Khan, not only about knowing him but about his movements after the Prague meeting, he was certain in his own mind that Andrews and Khan were responsible for the murders of Simone and Aline Lagarde. Or should that be the CIA and Pakistani intelligence?

'There's one more thing,' said Le Grice. 'When Khan left France he didn't fly to Pakistan.'

'No?'

'He boarded a flight to London.'

EIGHTEEN

Steven hadn't seen that coming. When he could think clearly again his initial thought was to put Khan at the top of the suspect list for the death of Tom North, but he reined in his imagination. It just wasn't possible to believe that the combined intelligence services of the UK, the US, France and Pakistan had colluded in the murders of two French medics and a prominent English scientist. That's what it looked like, but there had to be another explanation. Please God there was.

Steven pondered his next move with heightened feelings of apprehension. He'd been sure he'd identified the bad guys and was making progress, but Khan's coming to London after leaving Paris and the possibility – which still remained – of his having murdered Tom North was throwing him. He understood only too well that the less you knew or understood about your enemy the more vulnerable you became. It was an uncomfortable feeling. One thing was for sure, Khan's presence in London was enough to make him call a code red. He went back through to see Macmillan, who acceded to the request without question after hearing what Steven had learned from Le Grice.

The code red status entitled him not only to be armed but to have on call a range of other operational back-up services ranging from credit cards to forensic laboratory expertise. A number of consultants in a wide range of specialties under Home Office retainers could be called upon to give opinions. There would be a dedicated duty officer at the end of a phone twenty-four hours a day ready to deal with his every request without question and, not least, he would have Home Office authority to call on police assistance whenever and wherever he felt the need. Under normal conditions a request could be made for police assistance; under code red UK police forces were obliged to comply. As always, Steven hoped that he would not have to call on any of these things but it was a comfort to know they were there.

He paid a visit to the armourer and left with a Glock 23 pistol nestling in a shoulder holster under his left arm and a supply of .40 ammunition in his briefcase. He did so with a heavy heart. Walking the streets of London knowing he was armed always seemed like a betrayal of everything he believed in. He took great pride in living in a country where the police didn't carry guns; it suggested a degree of civilisation that set the UK apart.

There was also the question of how Tally would see it. His assertions about the largely routine nature of his investigations now seemed more like lies than the reassurances they were meant to be. He decided not to go back to the Home Office, returning instead to Marlborough Court where he got out the relevant files again and started looking for inspiration.

He took a sheet of A4 paper from the paper tray of his printer in the corner of the room and laid it on the table next to the files. 'Tabula rasa,' he murmured. A clean sheet . . . a new beginning. He wrote the word *Afghanistan* at the top and dropped a vertical line to where he added *Prague*.

He put *Simone* and *Aline* at the head of the list: they had set the ball rolling. Simone felt something had gone badly wrong with the vaccination effort against polio in north-west Pakistan and wanted to make her fears public. She'd been denied the chance in Prague by, among others, her own bosses, who knew about the presence of fake aid teams but had conspired to keep quiet because of the CIA's apology and a promise to put much more in the way of aid into the region.

All this, however, was political: it wasn't a reason for anyone to murder Simone and Aline, so there was something else, something to do with people falling sick in a remote Afghan village and blood samples that ended up in Porton Down.

A number of big players in the world of science and medicine had met in the Czech Republic to discuss their failure to wipe out polio in Pakistan's north-west frontier region. He wrote the names of these players next to *Prague*. Their involvement in the proceedings ended here. They had all agreed to keep quiet about the CIA's action in the belief that they were preventing a backlash against aid teams in general. It was understandable. These people had to live in the real world and act with pragmatism. To them, Simone would have been seen as a nuisance but nothing more. To others, she must have constituted a real threat.

Steven drew a short line down from *Prague* and pencilled in *Bill Andrews* and *Ranjit Khan*, adding in brackets after their names *CIA* and *Pakistani intelligence* respectively. They had a different reason for wanting to keep Simone quiet. She either knew something . . . or possessed something that they wanted? This was a new thought and one inspired by what had happened to Tom North. Had he been killed because Andrews and Khan had failed to get what they were looking for from Simone or Aline?

Steven drew a line down from *Prague* to *Paris* and wrote in Aline's name before moving on down to *London*. The only link between Simone and London was the series of blood samples she'd taken in the village and sent there. She'd posted them to the North lab but they had been redirected to Porton Down by Dan Hausman. Steven pencilled *Fort Detrick, CIA* and *Reeman Losch* against Hausman's name before drawing a line that looped out back up to *Prague* and the delegate attending from Porton, Neville Henson.

He took a moment before he wrote Ranjit Khan's name against *London*. Why had Khan come to London? It couldn't have been to stop the blood samples going anywhere for analysis: it was too late for that, and why would he need to do it anyway? Hausman, who was almost certainly CIA, was already in the North lab and had been able to divert them away from the diagnostic investigation that Simone had requested. He'd simply passed them on to Henson at Porton. When questioned, his explanation for redirecting the samples had been that they were obliged to forward samples from patients with undiagnosed conditions to a lab equipped to do diagnostic work. That was true, but he'd lied about where he'd actually sent them.

Tom North's torture and murder was still a puzzle, in terms of both who had done it and why. What did the killer want from him? He might have twigged what Hausman was involved in and threatened to expose him, or perhaps he had known nothing of what was going on in Afghanistan but had stumbled across something that had made him, suspicious . . . but what was that something? And why the torture element?

Steven acknowledged for the first time that he had been underestimating Hausman's role in all of this. He'd been so pleased to get Jean's findings linking him with Fort Detrick and the CIA that he hadn't given much thought to what he might actually be doing in the North lab in the first place. He'd just been thinking of him as the person who'd sent on some blood samples to Porton and lied about it. There had to be more to Hausman than that. The fact that he had sent them to a named individual at Porton suggested a personal connection which in turn suggested a possible link between the North lab and Fort Detrick and Porton and maybe even CDC Atlanta, considering the presence of one of their people at the Prague meeting.

Although Hausman had not volunteered much about what he was working on when Tom North had introduced them on his first visit to the lab, Steven remembered that North had told him that the American was working on post-polio syndrome, the puzzling condition developed in later years by some people who'd recovered from the disease in earlier life. Was that true? Or was it a cover for some giant conspiracy involving germ warfare labs on both sides of the Atlantic?

Steven turned his attention to Bill Andrews, the CIA-backed head of charity funding for aid teams in Afghanistan and Ranjit Khan's suspected accomplice in the murder of Simone. According to what he'd learned from people from WHO and *Médecins Sans Frontières*, Andrews was about to preside over a huge new injection of funds into the region – many more aid teams with American funding were going to appear on the ground. Was this really just conscience money from the CIA or was there something else behind it?

Steven had a eureka moment. He suddenly had a frightening vision of what was going on. A new biological weapon had been devised. Scientists at Porton Down and Fort Detrick and at least Hausman in the North lab had been involved in its development and MI6, the CIA and probably French and Pakistani intelligence were, to varying extents, in the know. The fact that a fake aid team had been discovered helping in the hunt for Bin Laden was small beer and had been used as a useful diversion.

There were other fake teams in the area and about to be a lot more. They weren't offering people protection; they were using the inhabitants of a remote, lawless region as experimental animals. That's why people were sick in the village that Simone and her team had stumbled across. They had been deliberately infected with something but . . . they were sick, not dead, Steven reminded himself. His hypothesis came to a grinding, pen-tapping halt.

He couldn't see a way round the problem. A few minutes ago he'd felt sure he'd cracked the mystery, but now . . . In the terrifying world of biological weaponry where tales of 'weaponised' anthrax and genetically altered smallpox conjured up visions of hell on earth with city streets filled with the dead and the dying, a weapon that made people sick didn't seem to rate. Was he missing something or was he simply wrong?

He wasn't prepared to abandon his line of thought just yet but he needed time – time without anyone rocking the boat was his next panic-driven thought. He suddenly saw Macmillan's plan to rattle cages in Whitehall by dropping Hausman's name and background into a conversation with the director of MI5 as counterproductive in the extreme and hurriedly called the Home Office.

'I'm sorry, he's gone to lunch, Steven,' said Jean Roberts.

Steven closed his eyes. That wasn't what he wanted to hear. 'How long ago did he leave?'

'About ten minutes. He's lunching at his club. He was walking over.'

Steven knew the walk across Green Park well enough: it took about ten minutes. 'Jean, can you use his emergency pager. Tell him not to mention Hausman to the director.'

'Not to mention Hausman . . . Consider it done.'

Steven smiled. Jean Roberts was never anything other than the epitome of efficiency. She confirmed a few minutes later that the message had been received and understood.

The relief Steven felt at having stopped Macmillan in time soon gave way to thoughts about what an alternative strategy might be. A more precise, clinical approach was called for but there seemed to be too many imponderables for that. He still felt that some sort of biological agent, developed in UK or US research labs, was key to the whole affair, but there was no obvious way of getting information about it. The important players were all scientists in top secret labs or members of the intelligence community – tough nuts to crack, but tough didn't necessarily mean impossible.

There was no question of getting anything out of anyone at Porton, one of the most secretive labs on earth, but Dan Hausman didn't work at Porton, he worked in a university lab, many of which were as secure as garden huts. He was CIA so it wouldn't be possible to scare him into talking, especially as there was nothing to threaten him with. On the other hand, if he had been working on the agent during his time in the North lab there should be some record of it – notes, lab books, records, computer files – maybe not lying around but somewhere in the building.

Now that Steven had managed to stop Macmillan Hausman would have no reason to believe that he was the subject of any kind of investigation. That was the way it should stay for the moment, at least until Steven was sure that the risks involved in making an unauthorised entry into the North lab could be justi-fied.

It still worried him that the proposed agent did not appear to be lethal and that he might be barking up the wrong tree, but considering the matter further brought to mind a conversation he'd had some years before with an expert on germ warfare. This particular professor had maintained that the time for the continual development of more and more lethal weapons had passed; there was a surfeit of them and the problem of infecting your own troops and population was still insurmountable. What was needed, the professor had asserted, were weapons that debilitated the enemy but could be reversed at a later stage. That way, military success could be achieved without lasting damage to property or personnel. Was this what he was dealing with here, the Holy Grail of bio-weaponry? It was something to bear in mind.

Steven turned his attention to Ranjit Khan but didn't get far. Khan was Pakistani intelligence and a killer and that was about it, apart from the highly relevant fact that he was currently here in London and was responsible for Steven's carrying the weapon sitting in the shoulder holster he'd hung over the corner of the chair opposite.

Bill Andrews, Khan's accomplice in the killing of Simone, was a different matter. He was American, CIA, and, with Khan, had probably been responsible for the introduction of fake teams in the first place. He was now about to use vastly increased funding to send in even more 'aid teams' to the region, ostensibly to step up the drive to eradicate polio but in reality – if Steven was right – to continue experiments with a new bio-weapon.

Steven remembered his earlier intention to ask Andrews about the dropped contact lens in the gallery of the Strahov library, but that was before Jean had discovered his CIA connection and exposed his lies about not knowing Khan and his whereabouts after the Prague meeting. It occurred to Steven that it might be an idea to take a step backwards and do just that – call up Andrews and ask about the contact lens. He had nothing to lose. It would reveal that he was still investigating Simone's death but nothing more than that and it might be interesting to hear what Andrews had to say. It might even tell him which one of the two had actually carried out the killing, not that they weren't both equally guilty in his eyes.

NINETEEN

A glance at the time and a quick calculation suggested it would be just after nine a.m. in Kansas City. Steven called the number Jean had given him and a young woman with a mid-western drawl answered with the name of the aid foundation, adding, 'My name is Cherry; how can I help you?'

Steven asked to speak to Andrews.

'Hey, you're not from round here.'

'I'm English.'

'Cool. Who shall I say is calling?'

Steven was told he'd be put on hold. He wasn't warned that the gap would be filled with country and western music. He waited patiently while a tale of family tragedy unfolded and a loved one ended up as a star in the sky before Andrews came on the line. 'Steven, this is an unexpected pleasure. How are you?'

'Very well, and you?'

'Real fine. What can I do for you?'

Steven latched on to the 'real fine' answer. It was not something he would have expected Andrews to say. The man was a preppy Harvard graduate but, Steven reminded himself, he was also CIA trained, a chameleon who would fit in wherever he happened to be. Currently he was in cowboy country. 'I'm sorry, Bill, but I'm still not clear about what happened in the gallery of the Strahov library. I was told someone lost a contact lens just before the accident. Have you any idea who that person might be?'

'I certainly have; it was me. One of my lenses got a bit out of place when I tilted my head back to look up at the ceiling and when I tried to correct the problem it came right out.'

'I see,' said Steven.

'Which is more than I could at the time,' joked Andrews. 'I got down on my hands and knees, imploring people around me to stand still in case they stepped on it. A few folk got down beside me, anxious to help, and there we all were on our knees. I made a joke about not knowing which way Mecca was and I heard Simone laugh. Then . . . the scream. My God, I still waken up in the night thinking about it.'

Steven took a moment to compose himself. He couldn't allow any hint of scepticism or anger to reach his voice. At least he now knew it was Khan who'd actually pushed Simone over the balustrade. Andrews had been conducting the diversionary pantomime on the floor at the time.

'Thanks, Bill. I think that answers my question.' Words were sticking in Steven's throat but he thought he should add a little small talk. 'I suppose you guys must be busy organising the new aid teams I heard about?'

'We sure are. I'll be coming to Europe next week to speak with the folks at Med Sans and the World Health Organisation about deployment. I'll be in London by Friday – maybe we could meet up and have a beer?'

'Look forward to it. Call me at the Home Office.'

So Andrews was coming to London, maybe for his given reason, maybe not, but both Simone and Aline's killers would be in the same place at the same time. He knew he shouldn't let things get personal but that might prove useful when it came to settling an outstanding score.

Time was getting on: Steven called the Home Office to see if John Macmillan was still there. He had yet to explain his request that he say nothing about Hausman at lunch.

'He is,' replied Jean. 'Shall I put you through?'

Steven said not. He'd come in and speak to him personally.

*　　*　　*

Macmillan listened to Steven in silence then got up to pour two sherries. Steven noted it was his best Amontillado, a sure sign he was impressed. He handed one to Steven, murmuring, 'A CIA cover-up masquerading as a CIA confession. Interesting.'

'I could be wrong.'

Macmillan sighed and said, 'When it comes to this kind of reasoning, Steven, I can't recall a single occasion in the past when you ever were. It's my fear that you won't be this time so let's make sure I'm understanding all this. You're proposing that there's a new bio-weapon, the brainchild of the British or the Americans or both, being tested on the unsuspecting hill tribes of the Pakistan/Afghanistan border under the guise of a vaccination programme. The CIA got caught out over one of the fake teams but managed to convince everyone it was gathering intelligence which led to the capture of Bin Laden – something that was true but not the whole story. They apologised profusely to all the genuine medical agencies in the region and everyone agreed to keep quiet because of the fear of destroying trust in the whole aid programme?'

Steven nodded. 'Just about covers everything.'

'There are times when I feel very old . . .'

Steven hid a smile.

'I can't fault the logic in anything you've said but, like you, I wonder about the non-lethal nature of the weapon . . .' He held up his hand when he saw Steven about to say something. 'You're going to point out that a weapon that incapacitates the enemy is very desirable – perhaps even more desirable than a killer – and I accept that. It's just that . . . you wouldn't think a weapon of that nature would warrant the degree of secrecy and cover-up we've been seeing. You might if it was some virus capable of unleashing Armageddon . . . but an incapacitator?'

Steven took Macmillan's point. 'So there must be more to it.'

Macmillan nodded. 'And the whole world's against us: there doesn't seem to be a damned soul we can ask.'

'True. We're on our own.'

Macmillan read more into Steven's comment than a statement of the obvious. 'And so?'

Steven admitted that he was considering an unauthorised entry into the lab where Dan Hausman worked. Macmillan raised his eyes. 'Now I wish I hadn't asked. You're sure there's no other way?'

'I can't see one. Like you say, we've got no friends.'

Macmillan got up to refill their glasses but Steven declined. 'I'm driving up to Leicester later.'

'Quite a commute.'

'Tally has an interview for a job in London coming up.' Steven told Macmillan about the post at Great Ormond Street.

'I wish her well.'

As Steven got up to go, Macmillan said, 'Correct me if I'm wrong, but I seem to remember you mentioning a PhD student in the North lab proving helpful when you were investigating what had happened to the blood samples?'

'Liam Kelly, yes. He was the one who told me what Hausman had really done with them.'

Macmillan posed the question by tilting his head to one side and opening his eyes a little wider.

Steven nodded. 'It's a good idea – I'm just not sure about involving him in something like this. He's only a boy . . . with a career to think about.'

'I wasn't thinking of any active role for him,' said Macmillan, 'more a case of an insider being able to offer a few helpful pointers about where things might be found . . . Have a think about it.'

Steven thought about little else on his way up to Leicester. Liam Kelly would know not only where Hausman worked – that much he knew already – but where his office space was located, which desk was his, his locker, his filing cabinet . . . but perhaps more important, Kelly would have an access key for the building and the lab. All PhD students in biological subjects needed out-of-hours access to their labs on a regular basis to follow the progress of experiments. It shouldn't put him at much risk to 'lose' it for a few hours. The decision to approach Kelly was made: it was a weight off his mind. That just left the problem of what he was going to say to Tally.

'Oh my God,' Tally exclaimed as she hugged Steven and withdrew quickly. 'I don't have to ask what's under your arm; I remember from last time. Oh, Steven . . .'

'It's just a precaution, Tally,' said Steven, knowing how weak it sounded. 'Just tell yourself every policeman in Europe carries one . . .'

'They do it routinely, you don't. There has to be a reason, a very good one and one I'm not going to like.'

'Look, the man I think killed Simone and Aline Lagarde is in London: we don't know why. As I say, it's just a precaution.'

Tally looked Steven straight in the eyes for a few silent moments before looking down at the floor and sighing. 'Sorry,' she said. 'I'm being unreasonable. I was the one who persuaded you to return to Sci-Med and now I'm making things difficult for you. You've got enough on your plate without me nagging at you. Forgive me?'

Steven made to take her in his arms but Tally put both hands against his chest. 'Not till you take that thing off.'

After a late supper they sat together on the couch, heads back, shoes off, feet up on a footstool, their toes flirting.

'I heard on the news there was another ME protest attack yesterday,' said Tally. 'A microbiologist in Edinburgh was sent a dead rat in the post.'

Steven grimaced. 'Not my problem any more,' he said. 'I've been taken off that investigation. John thinks I've got enough to do with the Afghanistan business. Scott Jamieson has taken over. D'you remember Scott?'

'We met at some point when John Macmillan was ill. Nice man, pretty wife, they live down in Kent. They invited us down as I remember.'

'Maybe we'll take them up on that when you get the job at Great Ormond Street. We'll wander hand in hand through the hop fields wondering what we're going to do with all the money you'll be making.'

'Let's not count our chickens.'

'It's in the bag.'

'Thursday,' said Tally.

'I'm sorry?'

'The interview. It's on Thursday. I wasn't going to tell you because I didn't want to distract you from the Afghanistan business, as you called it. Afghanistan,' sighed Tally, snuggling into Steven. 'What are we doing there? Iraq, Afghanistan, Libya. Our youngsters are out of work, our health service is falling to bits and we're strutting around on the world stage like we owned the place. One of our soldiers gets blown to bits every week and TV newsreaders look sad for five seconds before telling us *the family has been informed*. Well, that's all right then. What's it all about?'

'Ssh,' said Steven, eyes closed, his arm hugging Tally a little tighter. 'I could come out with some spiel about the war on terror, making our country a safer place, standing up for human rights, introducing democracy to the downtrodden masses, expanding the free world . . . but I don't believe any of that rubbish either. Money will be behind it, money and oil. It always is.

'Aren't you one of them?' asked Tally. 'The establishment, I mean?'

'What do you think?'

'I think I love you. I'm so glad I found you. I think I stopped feeling lonely the day I met you.'

Steven was taken aback at Tally's impromptu declaration but felt very pleased. He planted a kiss on her forehead and asked, 'Who's going to fetch the drinks?'

'You are.'

Steven returned with two gins and Tally smiled sleepily. Thinking about their conversation over supper, she asked, 'When you said Khan and Andrews were going to be in London . . . Do you have enough evidence to arrest them for Simone's murder?'

'No.'

'Promise me you're not considering taking matters into your own hands.'

'Don't be silly.'

'Steven?'

'There's a good chance the French police will come up with a DNA match to convict Khan and he'll probably shop Andrews to minimise his sentence.'

Tally looked at him accusingly. 'They're intelligence community people, not naughty schoolboys who stole sweeties from a corner shop.'

'They're not beyond the law.'

'It's whose law they're subject to I'm worried about.'

TWENTY

Jean Roberts looked surprised when she found Steven sitting in her office at ten minutes to nine on Monday morning. 'Don't tell me, you had a fight with Tally and you've been here all night?'

'No. Well not yet, anyway,' Steven replied. 'I'd like you to get some information for me as soon as you can. I need to know what the City College authorities have decided about Tom North's group. Is it still functioning as a research group or has it been broken up? I'm particularly interested in Dr Dan Hausman and a PhD student named Liam Kelly. I need you to do it as discreetly as possible: I don't want to advertise our interest, particularly not to Hausman.'

Jean looked up from the pad she'd been noting things down on. 'I'll make an approach through their administration. I'll pretend I'm from one of the grant-funding bodies making a routine check.'

'Perfect,' said Steven. 'I also need to make contact with Liam Kelly but I don't want to turn up at the lab. An address for him would be good.'

'What year is he?' asked Jean.

'First year PhD, just about to start his second.'

'If I were a first year PhD student who'd just lost my supervisor, I think I would be spending a lot of time in the library boning up on things that might make me attractive to other potential supervisors.'

'Jean, you're a genius.'

Jean demurred with a modest little smile. 'I'll still get you the information. Coffee?'

Steven got to City College library just before noon. He showed his Sci-Med ID to the librarian and told her he needed to check some things in an early edition of the *Journal of General Virology* which his usual library didn't have. The implication of bibliographic superiority seemed to please the woman, who directed him across the room with the end of her pen.

Steven extracted one of the heavy, bound volumes, placed it on a nearby table and opened it, taking care to give the impression he was looking for a specific article before sitting down and taking out a notebook from his briefcase.

When people in the vicinity stopped taking a casual interest in the newcomer Steven started taking an interest in them, but found no familiar faces among the students and staff he could see from where he was sitting. Periodically he would get up and return to the sliding bookshelf area where he would remove a volume and pretend to search through the pages while really looking through the gaps on the shelves at other areas of the library. After his second such sortie, he spotted Liam Kelly sitting at a study carrel with his back to him.

Still carrying one of the volumes, Steven walked over and tapped Liam on the shoulder, saying in a low voice, 'I thought it was you. How are you doing?'

Liam turned and looked up. 'Oh, hi. I'm okay. What are you doing here?'

'Looking for you, actually,' Steven confessed. 'Do you think we could have a word?'

Liam looked vaguely uncertain. 'Maybe this isn't the best place for a conversation?'

The look being given to them by a serious-looking young girl in the neighbouring carrel added weight to this assertion. Steven offered up an apologetic smile and said to Liam, 'C'mon, I'll buy you lunch.'

Once out into the noise of the traffic, he asked if Liam knew a good pub in the area.

'The Talisman's okay.'

'Lead on.'

It was early; they had no trouble finding a corner table where sunlight played on a painting up on the wall of Nelson's ship at Trafalgar. Steven sipped a Czech lager and asked, 'Any word about your future?'

Liam wiped the Guinness froth from his top lip and replied, 'It's all a bit of a mess at the moment. I was really into the project I had with Tom so I'm reluctant to stray too far from it, but I can see the point of other supervisors who'd want me to work on something they're interested in. Apart from that, funding's going to be a problem. I've used up a whole year of my three-year grant and there's no way of getting that back if I were to start out on something new.'

Steven nodded. 'How about the others in the group?'

'At the moment, we've been told to carry on as normal but that's just to give the suits time to decide what they're going to do about us. Mind you, I heard one of them say to Dan Hausman that his position had been "stabilised", whatever that meant.'

I'll bet it has, thought Steven. The intelligence services would have seen to that.

'So what is it you wanted to see me about?' asked Liam.

Steven paused to let the waitress put down the plates she'd arrived with. She smiled. 'Can I get any sauces for you?'

Steven shook his head. Liam asked for ketchup.

'Do you remember telling me where Dan had sent the blood samples I was interested in when he had a . . . lapse of memory?'

'Sure.'

'You remembered the name of the person he'd sent them to, Dr Neville Henson.'

'That's right. I saw the label.'

'Did you see the address?'

Liam smiled and put down his fork. He'd been eating American style with fork only. 'So that's what this is about. Sure I did. It was Porton Down.'

'I take it you know what that place is all about?'

Liam smiled. 'It's our defence establishment . . . keeps us all safe.'

'Didn't it strike you as odd?'

'Lots of things struck me as odd in Tom's lab. That was just one more.'

This was music to Steven's ears. 'Good. I want to hear about all of them, starting with what you thought when you saw the Porton address.'

Liam sighed before saying, 'I suppose I thought the blood samples must contain something dangerous if they were being referred to a place like Porton.'

'Did you have any other reason to think that?'

Liam moved his head from side to side to indicate uncertainty. 'I've thought for some time that something strange has been going on in the lab, ever since Dan arrived.'

'Like what?'

'Dan didn't behave like your usual new post-doc – I mean a bit deferential and that. It was as if he was Tom's equal, if you know what I mean. The pair of them definitely had something going on.'

'And you've no idea what?'

Liam shook his head. 'No, but I got the impression that Dan had discovered something important and the pair of them were keeping it a secret from the rest of us. Normally, we would have had a group meeting about who was doing what and we'd all have our say but that didn't happen. Outsiders used to come to the lab, though, guys in suits, and talk to Tom and Dan in private. The rest of us used to josh Dan about it but he never said what it was all about.'

'Dan is CIA,' said Steven, judging the moment to be right.

Liam paused while taking a mouthful, leaving his fork in mid-air. 'Fuck's sake,' he whispered. 'You're kidding me.'

'He came to you via a fake pharmaceutical company used by our American cousins after having worked at Fort Detrick – the American Porton.'

Liam lost interest in his food and sat shaking his head.

The waitress appeared. 'Is everything all right for you?' she inquired.

Steven gave her a quick smile. 'Very nice.'

Liam looked up at Steven. 'And now the million dollar question: why are you telling me this?'

'I need your help. I want to know what's been going on in the North lab and, if you're right, I want to know what it is that Dan has discovered.'

Liam chose to resume eating while he considered and Steven did likewise.

'All finished?' asked the waitress. Both men sat back to let her clear the table. 'Will you be requiring any sweets or coffees?'

'Espresso for me,' said Steven.

Liam opted for the same. He could see that Steven was waiting for a response but he was struggling to put his thoughts into words. 'If Dan is CIA and Porton Down is involved, then surely our governments know exactly what's been going on. I mean, it's their thing. Where exactly do you come in? What's it got to do with Sci-Med?'

'I need you to trust me.'

The cloud of suspicion darkened.

'Our government *thinks* it knows what's been going on . . . but it doesn't. I think they're being played for a patsy.'

Liam took a deep breath and sat back as the coffee arrived. 'And so they need Dr Steven Dunbar of the Sci-Med Inspectorate to put them right?'

'I also have a personal interest,' said Steven, putting his final card on the table, hoping it would capture Liam's interest. 'Somewhere in this whole mess someone thought it was a good idea to murder my friend Simone Ricard, the aid worker who sent you the blood samples. It's my intention to show them . . . it really wasn't.'

Liam took note of the look on Steven's face. 'Well, I'm fucking glad it wasn't me,' he murmured before taking a sip of his coffee. 'All right,' he said quietly. 'Count me in.'

Steven relaxed a little and sipped his own coffee. 'I can't promise you the PhD placement of your dreams,' he said, 'but you won't have any grant money problems, I promise. Sci-Med will see to that.'

'Cheers. Sci-Med doesn't exactly do things by the book, does it?'

'Let's say we cherish our independence.'

'What is it you want me to do?'

'I'll need access to your lab out of hours and I need advice about where to look to get information about what Hausman has been up to. I'm assuming Tom North's stuff will have been cleared out?'

'The suits did that quite quickly. Why don't you let me have a sniff around? I'm better placed than anyone else.'

'Because I don't want you doing anything that could damage your career . . . or worse.'

Liam was left to dwell on what 'worse' might be for a few moments. 'Maybe you're right,' he agreed, 'but I'll keep my ears and eyes open. By the way, it may be irrelevant but blood samples weren't the only thing your friend Simone sent in the package to the lab.'

'Really?'

'There was a computer disk and a note saying that she'd explain when she came to the lab – I think she'd arranged to see Tom the week after she died. I heard Tom tell Dan that he'd had a look but couldn't make head or tail of it; it was gobbledegook. To be honest neither of them seemed that fussed. I remember it was in an envelope marked *Vaccination schedules.*'

Steven's pulse rate rose dramatically. 'Do you know what happened to the disk?' he asked.

Liam shook his head slowly. 'I think Dan was the last to take a look at it. Maybe he still has it. If he gave it back to Tom, it will probably have been cleared out with the rest of his stuff. Why? Is it important?'

'It wasn't gobbledegook. It was encrypted. She sent a memory card to me. I think it's probably the key.'

'Jesus, but why would anyone go to the trouble of encrypting vaccination schedules?'

'Who knows?' said Steven.

'I could have a look around for the disk if you like,' said Liam. 'I mean neither Tom nor Dan seemed to think anything of it so it's probably not under lock and key.'

'Don't take any risks, but if it does happen to be lying around . . . Look, I've kept you long enough,' said Steven, signalling to the waitress for the bill. 'Give me your mobile number and I'll be in touch when I've come up with a plan. If I suggest a meeting, assume it's here or just outside if it's not during opening hours. Here's my mobile number: let me know if you have any luck with the disk or if there's anything you think I should be aware of.'

TWENTY-ONE

Steven left Liam and headed off to walk by the river. He was glad that he now had help on the inside, and the revelation about the disk was exciting. If Simone had thought it necessary to keep the disk and its key separate, she might have suspected there was more to it than vaccination schedules. Alternatively, she might simply have assumed that the disk and the card were copies of the same information – proof of faulty vaccination practices – and she'd kept them separate because she'd been unsure about whom among her colleagues she could trust.

Despite making good progress he started to feel very uneasy about what he was planning next. It wouldn't be the first time he'd crossed the line of what was strictly legal in the course of an investigation – sometimes it was unavoidable – but this time it was different. It was just . . . downright stupid. That was the depressing conclusion he reached as he leaned on the embankment wall to take in the view.

Below him, about thirty metres away, a man in a knitted hat was sweeping the exposed low-tide mud with a metal detector, wholly captivated by the prospect of unearthing buried treasure. Steven couldn't help but see the parallel. He'd been planning an unauthorised entry to a university lab to search for the answer to a puzzle but there was something that he'd been failing to properly acknowledge. He was seeking to uncover a secret that the governments of the UK and the US and their intelligence services didn't want him to know. Was he out of his mind? He had to be if he really believed he was going to find it lying around. The guy with the metal detector had more chance of coming up with the Koh-i-Noor.

Steven was tempted to abandon all thoughts of a break-in, either assisted or unassisted, but steeled himself to go on thinking things through from every angle as he'd done so often in the past. At last he thought he might have found a loophole. The work that Hausman was doing might be top secret but it wasn't being carried out in a top security lab like those you'd find at Fort Detrick or Porton Down. Why not? Because . . . the North lab was a more suitable place for the work . . . but this had to be for scientific not security reasons. That was the compromise that must have been made. The North lab must have expertise that was relevant to the work. There was a connection with polio.

Steven felt a little better. His conclusion fitted well with what Liam had told him about Tom North's being in on what was going on – something he'd been unsure about. It also made sense because he would have had to agree at some point to taking Hausman into his lab, although perhaps he'd been under some government pressure to do so.

Unfortunately, according to Liam North's office had been cleared out so any carelessness an academic might have shown in record keeping or file storage couldn't be exploited. Hausman was a different kettle of fish. He was CIA; it would be second nature for him to cover his tracks.

Steven cursed under his breath as he seemed to be back where he started . . . but he wasn't. Hausman might be rock solid but the lab *and its resources* weren't. Hausman would have had to use – and still be using – the university computer system, its servers and IT provisions. Could this be the Achilles heel he was looking for?

Next day Steven talked things through with John Macmillan. 'With a bit of luck we might still be able to access some of Tom North's stuff on the university computer system as well as have a go at accessing stuff from Hausman.'

'You mean on their servers and back-up systems?'

'Precisely.'

Macmillan nodded. 'So how do we go about doing it? It'll require a high degree of computer expertise . . . which gives us a bit of a dilemma. Under normal circumstances we'd just call in expert assistance from one or more of our consultants . . .'

'But in this case we can't because we'd be soliciting their help in committing an illegal act,' Steven completed.

'An illegal act against our own government. Difficult.'

Both men sat in silence with the distant sounds of London traffic appearing to become louder because of the quiet in the room. Eventually, Macmillan posed a question. 'We've been assuming that all the authorities are in on this secret. Can you think of one that isn't?'

Steven thought back to the meeting they'd had with the Foreign Secretary and heads of the security services. Who was present . . . and who wasn't. 'The police?' he ventured.

'The police,' Macmillan repeated with a smile. 'It's my guess that someone decided that London's boys in blue didn't need to know what was going on.'

'Maybe time for a lunch with Charlie?' Steven suggested. He was referring to Chief Superintendent Charles Malloy, a friend of Macmillan's who had been helpful to Sci-Med in the past. Steven knew and liked him too. He was his own man and didn't always go by the book – maybe something that had denied him access to the very top of the career pole.

Macmillan nodded. 'We'll have to be very clear about what we're asking of him. It could be his head on the block as well as ours.'

Steven agreed.

'So what are we asking?'

'Supposing the police had some reason to enter City College and confiscate computer equipment . . . lots of it,' suggested Steven.

'What reason did you have in mind?'

'Porn.'

Macmillan raised his eyebrows.

'As bad as it gets. We find a way to plant the stuff on their system and tip off the police. Once we have the gear, Charlie lets our experts examine everything only it won't be porn we'll be looking for.'

'The "planting" bit makes me nervous,' said Macmillan. 'Charlie would have to agree to it from the outset.'

'Of course,' Steven said. 'In fact, I was thinking, maybe he might come up with the material we need. You know, stuff confiscated by the police? I mean, I don't think I could convince Tally I was working at home without sustaining grievous bodily harm.'

'Lady Macmillan might not be too amused either,' said Macmillan. 'I'll ask Jean.'

'For porn?'

'To set up lunch as soon as possible.'

Steven decided to say nothing to Liam about the proposal until Macmillan had approached Charlie: he now knew that would be on Thursday. It promised to be a big day for more than one reason, as Tally would be interviewed for the Great Ormond Street job then. She was taking two days' leave and would travel to London on Wednesday, staying overnight with him at Marlborough Court before returning to Leicester after the interview to be on duty first thing on Friday morning.

That left Wednesday as a bit of a limbo day. Steven passed the morning cleaning and tidying the flat and thinking about how they might 'infect' the City College computer system, assuming Charlie Malloy agreed to the plan – and the more he thought about that the less likely it seemed. He hadn't come to any conclusion by the time Tally arrived and admired his efforts.

Steven found her looking out of the window when he brought coffee through from the small kitchen. 'Penny for them,' he said.

'I was wondering what it would be like to live here,' she replied.

'And?'

'I think it would be just fine.'

They set off for lunch 'somewhere in the country' in accordance with Tally's request when he'd spoken to her the night before – 'Somewhere where I can take in great breaths of clean, fresh air without the remotest suggestion of hospital smells.'

Steven had decided to put aside thoughts of work for the day and offer Tally his full support, although it did occur to him as they drove out of town, heading for the south coast, that the fact that Liam hadn't contacted him yet probably meant he'd failed to locate the disk.

'How are you feeling?' he asked when they'd placed their order at the country pub he'd decided on.

'Exactly how you think I'm feeling,' Tally replied with a wry smile. 'I think I may have over-reached myself in applying for this one.'

'Nonsense. You couldn't do any such thing. You're the best. I keep telling you that.'

'You do and I thank you for it but I think I'm the realistic one in this duo. I mean, Great Ormond Street, what was I thinking of?'

'You'll see tomorrow. Your references will be fantastic and they'll see in you exactly what they're looking for: an outstanding physician who cares deeply about her patients – to the extent that she refuses to take a holiday even when the job is threatening her health.'

'Let's not go there. There's nothing wrong with my health,' Tally growled.

'Nothing that a holiday wouldn't cure.'

'Dunbar!'

The waitress, a pleasant Australian girl who was 'doing Europe', returned with their food and interrupted what Tally was about to say. Tally and Steven sat looking at each other while the plates were placed before them, Tally adopting a mock threatening expression while Steven favoured a smug, schoolboy grin.

'Things will be easier when you're a consultant,' said Steven, continuing with the tease. 'We'll be going away all the time.'

'Are you going to stop this?'

'Mind you, in my experience, there are certain things you'll have to do if you hope to be accepted as a real medical consultant.'

'Like what?'

'Wear red trousers and a bow tie, adopt a very loud voice and play golf.'

Tally couldn't stop herself laughing. 'You're impossible,' she said.

TWENTY-TWO

By Thursday evening Liam Kelly was disappointed that he hadn't heard anything more from Steven Dunbar. Over the past twenty-four hours he had undergone a change of heart. His initial reluctance to become involved in anything not entirely above board had been replaced by the seductive thought that he might actually be entering the world of spies and secrets; Bond film territory. He recognised it was a bit soon to be changing from Guinness in the students' union to vodka martinis at the Ritz – damn, he couldn't remember if they should be stirred or shaken – but to a 22-year-old red-blooded male the idea of being part of a scenario involving top secret defence establishments, the CIA and classified research was proving very exciting indeed.

Maybe if his association with Steven were to go well, a position with Sci-Med might even be a possibility – after he'd finished his PhD, of course. His research was still important to him, and up until now he hadn't even considered an alternative to a career in academia, but it wouldn't do any harm to widen his horizons a little.

Steven had mentioned at one point that all Sci-Med investigators had to be well qualified in either science or medicine so he was on track there. He didn't know what other qualifications were required but he could see himself presenting his ID, just as Steven had done . . . the embossed government crest . . . the photograph . . . Dr L. Kelly, Her Majesty's Sci-Med Inspectorate. Pulling power or what?

Liam put aside the scientific paper he'd been reading; new work on viral receptors had momentarily become less intriguing than wondering how he might speed things up in his other 'mission'. He'd managed to sneak a look through the stuff on the shelves above Dan Hausman's desk that very afternoon but without success. There had been no sign of the disk but he'd had to hurry as there were others around in the lab and any one of them might have come into the small office area at any moment. His heart had been pounding and he'd felt physically sick when doing it – perhaps not the best of starts to his new career, but lost ground might be recovered if he were to go back to the lab tonight and conduct a more thorough search. He would don a pair of surgical gloves and work his way through the drawers of Dan's desk.

Steven could not fail to be impressed if he were to turn up with the disk and casually hand it over. It would be a big step in the right direction. He could even see them having a celebratory drink afterwards, just a couple of guys who'd outwitted the CIA in the interests of Her Majesty's Government. He put on his denim jacket, checked the back pocket of his jeans for his lab card-key and told his flatmate he was 'going out for a bit'.

Despite having gone into the lab after hours many times before, tonight seemed distressingly different for Liam. He felt nervous, he felt anxious, but most of all he felt guilty. The night was full of eyes, watching him and reading the sign *up to no good* he felt must be tattooed on his forehead. He hated himself for feeling that way – even his palms were sweaty as he inserted his card-key into the lock and stabbed in his code with his index finger. He didn't realise that this was the way most normal, law-abiding citizens would feel in a situation like this – about to knowingly do wrong with possible serious consequences.

The darkened entrance hall did have lighting but only dim night-lights that seemed to magnify the size and imagined malevolence of the shadows as Liam made his way to the lifts. He was glad he was wearing trainers: they were quiet and didn't echo. The lift machinery ground into action and a car started its descent, immediately making him wonder why it wasn't at ground level in the first place. Someone must have recently gone up in it.

So what? said the voice of common sense inside his head. Lots of people came and went at all hours of the day and night in a place like this. It was a research institute for God's sake. Research wasn't a nine till five job. He knew that and yet . . . Someone had been smoking in the lift was his first thought as he stepped inside and pressed the button. Not allowed, definitely not allowed. Mind you, it could have been someone who'd been smoking outside the building and the smell had still been clinging to their clothes. Shit, he'd gone from being 007 to working for Health and Safety.

The lift stopped and, for a moment, Liam considered going right back down again and making a run for home. His flirtation with the world of shadows and adrenalin rushes was over. This really wasn't his thing; he was a nervous wreck. A life in academia would be just fine. The world of woolly sweaters and bicycles, seminars and blackboards beckoned him back.

He held down the 'door open' button for a full five seconds before finally overcoming his angst and stepping out over the threshold. It's your own lab, man; you've every right to be here, said the voice of reason. Don't be a complete girl's blouse. He managed a brave but tuneless whistle as he walked along the corridor to the lab. There it was again, a vague smell of tobacco.

As he reached the frosted glass swing doors to the North lab, he imagined a change in the darkness inside, a change that he couldn't quite put his finger on but had to ascribe to the blue funk he was in. The lights weren't on inside but the many windows allowed in light from neighbouring buildings and the street lights below. He turned on the lab lights and paused while the fluorescent strips stuttered into life. The lab looked just like it always did.

Liam walked over to his bench and lit the Bunsen burner. He wanted to create the suggestion of a reason for his being here should a security man look in. He perched on his stool, taking comfort for a moment from the sound and warmth of the burner flame and the air of normality it was providing. He shook his head and just couldn't understand his nerves. What an idiot.

Liam got together a series of bits and pieces of lab glassware and a bottle of culture medium. He really would set up a few cultures before he left just in case anyone should suspect that he'd been in and ask about it. With that done, he took out a pair of latex gloves from the box above his bench and put them on as he walked towards the closed door of the side room where Dan had his desk.

Liam wrinkled his nose as competing smells reached him; one was that damned tobacco smell again and the other was . . . human vomit. He put his hand to his face – adding latex to the mix – and stopped in his tracks. What the hell was going on? His nerves had returned like a swift incoming tide. Was he really smelling these things or was tension screwing up his senses?

Once again he was tempted to turn and head for home but the office door was only a metre away and his bench alibi looked just fine – as if he'd been working for the past thirty minutes. Five minutes more and he'd be done searching through the drawers. Surely he could hold himself together that long? Of course he could.

Liam opened the office door and light from the main lab entered to reveal a tableau from hell. An Asian man was standing there, pointing a pistol fitted with a silencer at him. Slumped in his desk chair and secured with tape was Dan Hausman. His face, swollen and distorted, spoke of the agony he was clearly in; a pool of vomit where he'd thrown up lay at his feet. Liam felt sickness well up in his own throat.

'Come inside. Shut the door behind you,' said Dr Ranjit Khan of Pakistani intelligence.

Liam did as he was told.

'Sit down in the other chair, back to me.'

Once again Liam complied. His fear was such that he had difficulty controlling his limbs and his mind was rebelling against taking in any more horror, but he could now see that the damage to Hausman's face and bare chest where his shirt had been ripped open had not been done by beating. The thick glass bottle on the desk and the glass dropper beside it testified to that. Smoke was curling up from the neck of the open bottle. Liam recognised the swimming baths smell – the fumes of hydrochloric acid. Hausman's left cheek was blistering badly and his lower lip was already deformed.

Liam struggled to say something and Khan hit him sharply across the back of his neck with the side of his hand, a blow hard enough to stun him and make sure that he was only vaguely aware of being trussed up with tape like Hausman. When he struggled back into full consciousness his assailant asked, 'Who the hell are you?'

'Liam Kelly . . . I'm a student.'

'Your colleague here has something I want, Mr Kelly. He's being rather awkward about it. But then he's CIA . . . all that training.'

'CIA?' exclaimed Liam, hoping that somewhere in his croaking reply, surprise had registered.

'I keep telling you . . .' groaned Hausman through burnt lips, 'I don't have the damned key . . .'

'Of course you do,' said Khan with a calm assurance that Liam found chilling. 'You're a credit to your service, but perhaps you'll feel differently about things when you watch me trickle acid slowly down Mr Kelly's forehead and see it enter his eyes.'

Liam lost control of his bladder sphincter as his head was jerked back by the hair and Khan filled the pipette with acid. 'Aren't you CIA chaps supposed to protect the innocent? Or is that just so much American crap, the sort of stuff your president spouts every time he steps in front of a camera?'

'He hasn't got it,' said Liam, his voice becoming a scream, having risen a full octave. 'It didn't come here. Dr Ricard sent it somewhere else.'

Khan seemed surprised. 'What the hell do you know about this?'

'Not much,' Liam gasped as his head was jerked back further. 'Just that she sent the key you're looking for to a friend.' He couldn't take his eyes off the glass dropper and its contents. It was being held about six inches from his face. The fumes from the open bottle of acid on the desk were already attacking his nasal mucosa.

'What friend?'

'Dr Steven Dunbar of the Sci-Med Inspectorate.'

'Where do you fit into the picture?'

'Steven has the key; he doesn't have the disk.'

'So he asked you to get it?'

'Sort of.'

'That's why you're here?'

'Yes.'

'What's Dunbar's interest?'

'Dr Ricard was his friend. He doesn't believe her death was an accident.'

Khan didn't comment but he put down the dropper and replaced the top on the acid bottle. 'Is that his only interest?'

'Yes.'

'Why did he want the disk?'

'If Dr Ricard sent him the encryption key, he thought she must have had a reason.'

Khan nodded, seemingly satisfied.

Liam could see that Hausman was losing consciousness. He desperately needed medical help. Liam said so to Khan.

'Indeed,' Khan agreed. 'Where do I find Dunbar?'

'I don't know.'

Khan looked sceptical. 'So how did you plan to tell him if you'd been successful?'

'He gave me a phone number.'

'Give me it.'

'It's on my phone.'

Khan removed Liam's mobile from the pocket of his denim jacket and flicked through Contacts. 'Steven D?'

'That's him.'

Khan nodded and picked up his pistol, which he'd laid down while he held Liam. He checked the tightness of the silencer before shooting both men through the back of the head.

TWENTY-THREE

It had been a bad day, Steven decided. He'd been harbouring notions of some kind of double celebration at the end of it with Tally being told she'd got the job at Great Ormond Street and Charlie Malloy agreeing to the scheme that was going to see progress in the investigation at a rate of knots. Instead, Tally had turned up at the flat at four thirty, feeling less than optimistic about her chances after a long day of interviews which she thought hadn't gone well. 'I think maybe I let my tongue run away with me on more than one occasion,' she reported. 'And I'm pretty sure I didn't say what they wanted to hear.'

Steven had tried reassuring her that they wouldn't be looking for a subservient, box-ticking wimp as one of their consultants, that they'd welcome a woman with strong views and a sense of what was right rather than what was politic, but failed to convince even himself. They both knew the establishment tended to prefer people who 'fitted in', people who, like the royal family, tended to avoid expressing views on anything.

Tally had set off back to Leicester. She'd let the evening rush hour pass before saying goodbye with an attempt at being cheerfully philosophical about what she feared would turn out be failure. There had been an underlying despondency about her, however, that Steven had found infectious. He poured himself a drink and slumped down in his favourite chair to put his heels up on the window sill. Feeling that she'd enough to worry about, he hadn't mentioned to Tally that he himself had a reason for feeling low. John Macmillan had returned from lunch with the news that

Charlie Malloy had dismissed their plan out of hand. 'Plain bloody lunacy,' he'd called it.

Steven had to smile; he couldn't help but see the funny side of it. It had been his idea and Malloy was probably right, but Macmillan had been the one to suffer the brunt of the policeman's attack on the 'bloody madness' of expecting the Met to plant porn on university computers in order to seize them and hand them over for examination. What was he thinking of? Macmillan had confessed to feeling like a naughty schoolboy being dressed down in the headmaster's study by the time Malloy was finished. The thought of silver-haired mandarin John Macmillan standing with head bowed, nervously examining his shoes while biting his lip, brought another smile from Steven and a slight shake of the head.

So where did they go from here? He still hadn't heard anything back from Liam so he had to assume that the boy had drawn a complete blank in trying to locate the disk. Another possible avenue had closed. He made a mental note to contact Liam the next day to arrange a meeting. Maybe searching through Hausman's stuff in the middle of the night really was becoming the only option – another depressing thought.

He turned on the TV and flicked through the channels looking for diversion. A documentary on fishing failed to excite, as did a programme on house renovation. A few seconds of an 'alternative' comedian only made him realise how much he missed Morecambe and Wise. Maybe it was the way he was feeling but nothing appealed for more than half a minute. Conceding defeat before his thumb grew tired, he made coffee and put Stan Getz on the stereo instead, only to find that *Jazz Samba* seemed totally at odds with the sound of rain battering on his window. He waited up until he'd heard from Tally that she was home safe, and turned in.

Steven's hopes of a good night's sleep to put an end to his day of frustration and disappointment and set him up for the challenges of a brand new dawn were doomed to disappointment. He tossed and turned as elements of both his investigative and his personal life swirled around in the margins between sleep and consciousness like pieces in a weightless jigsaw, all stubbornly refusing to click into any cohesive picture. It was almost a relief when his phone insisted he wake up at three a.m. It was John Macmillan.

'I've just had Charlie Malloy on the phone. Two bodies have been discovered by night security at City College.'

Steven was suddenly very wide awake. Knowing that he wasn't going to like the answer, he asked, 'Do we know who?'

'Dan Hausman and Liam Kelly.'

Steven felt a tsunami of conflicting emotions engulf him. 'Oh, Christ.' He was already playing out a scenario where Liam had taken the investigation of Hausman into his own hands and been caught in the act. Somehow, in the resulting altercation, both men had died.

Macmillan stopped his imagination in its tracks. 'Both were shot. Charlie thinks a pro job, back of the head.'

Steven was attempting to think up a new scenario when a sudden thought diverted him and he asked, 'Why did Charlie call *you*?'

'Because he's a nice man,' replied Macmillan. 'He saw the opportunity to help us out despite his earlier misgivings about our sanity. His boys will remove every bit of computer equipment they can lay their hands on, ostensibly as part of their murder investigation. They're doing that right now. He said he's got a feeling that official shutters are going to come down on these killings as soon as MI5 and their pals get their act together. Charlie will let us know where and when we can access the computers just as soon as he can. I'll see about calling in a couple of our consultants. I take it you'll make yourself available to brief them on what they're looking for?'

'Of course,' said Steven. He recognised that this was a big step forward but Liam Kelly's death was stopping him from sounding enthusiastic. 'It had to be Khan,' he said. He was trying to think logically but thoughts of Liam kept intruding. Liam was little more than a boy, a bright student at the very outset of his career with everything to live for, and now he was dead . . . *thanks to him.* The accusation was loud and clear. If he hadn't approached Liam, none of this would have happened. Live with that, Dunbar, if you can.

Macmillan picked up on a few muttered expletives at the other end of the phone. 'Are you all right?' he asked.

Steven ignored the question. 'Did Charlie have anything else to say about the deaths?'

'Quite a bit, none of it good. Hausman was tortured. Acid was involved.'

Steven screwed up his face as the horror level kept rising. 'So Khan wanted something . . . or wanted to know something . . . but he's Pakistani intelligence. He knows what's been going on,' he argued.

'Maybe not everything,' said Macmillan. 'Pakistan's a mess. No one knows who to trust in government. The political parties loathe each other and no one's sure what the army has in mind. The intelligence services are fractured and probably pursuing their own agenda, while the Americans are reluctant to tell them anything they don't have to know. That's how they got to Bin Laden. There are those who say that if the Pakistani government had been told in advance of the operation, Bin Laden would have disappeared like snow in July.'

Steven nodded and took everything on board. 'So it's possible Khan knows something but not everything.'

'But he wants to know everything . . . badly.'

'And Liam?' Steven asked in trepidation.

'It's cold comfort, I know, but there was no sign of torture.'

Steven was ready to snatch at any crumb of comfort that was offered. 'Thank God,' he said. 'Khan must have accepted that Liam didn't know anything.'

'Possibly, or maybe Liam appeared on the scene later, maybe even by accident, by which time Hausman had told Khan what he wanted to know,' Macmillan suggested.

Steven wanted to embrace this suggestion with all his heart: the idea that Liam had gone into the lab for some reason unconnected with this whole sorry business – maybe something to do with his research – and had come across Khan and Hausman by accident was exactly what he wanted to believe, but . . . There was always a but. 'You said Dan Hausman was tortured. Did Charlie say . . . how badly?'

'He was a real mess. His face was practically unrecognisable according to Charlie.'

'So he must have held out for quite some time . . . or couldn't tell Khan what he wanted to know . . . because he didn't know himself . . . and Khan didn't believe him.'

Both men imagined this nightmare situation for a few moments.

'Charlie said the bodies were discovered during a routine security patrol in the small hours,' said Macmillan. 'By that time, Khan was long gone. That suggests he wasn't interrupted during his interrogation. The fact that he executed both men at the end of it suggests strongly that he did get what he wanted.'

'Unless, of course, it was Liam who disturbed him and panicked him into giving up and leaving?'

Macmillan knocked that idea on the head. 'Charlie says both men were found tied to chairs in a small office. He'd been questioning them both.'

'Okay, so he wasn't disturbed,' said Steven, sounding resigned.

Macmillan read his mind. 'I think we have to accept that Khan now knows what we don't.

Steven took this as a gentle reminder that he focus on the matter in hand and not dwell on things he could do nothing about, like Liam's death and how much he might be to blame. He took a deep breath and said, 'We'll need copies of the PM reports, particularly ballistics. We can ask Le Grice in Paris to check them against the bullet used to kill Aline Lagarde.'

'Let's get a couple of hours' sleep,' said Macmillan.

Steven knew this was not possible in his case. He made some strong coffee and went over in his mind all that had happened.

The flat was quiet, deathly quiet, a bit like the mortuary Liam Kelly's body would be lying in, a cold, white sheet covering the unruly red hair and the face that had smiled so much in life. Awful, absolutely bloody awful, but at least he hadn't suffered the hellish torture that Hausman had been put through . . . because . . . because . . . Steven ran through the possible reasons again. Liam was a student; he wouldn't know anything about any top secret work going on in the lab . . . Hausman had finally broken and told Khan what he wanted to know . . . No, no, no, this was all wrong. Oh, so wrong.

'Oh, Christ,' murmured Steven as the truth dawned on him and sent a chill down his spine. Hausman hadn't told Khan what he wanted to know, Liam had. It wasn't information Khan had been after; it was the disk and encryption key that Simone had sent. The disk had nothing to do with vaccination schedules – that's why it had been encrypted in the first place. Khan knew what was on the disk but no one in the North lab did and no one in the North lab knew that the encryption key existed. They had dismissed the disk as being damaged or irrelevant or both. The only person who knew that the disk was encrypted and who had the key was Liam. The bottom line had to be that Liam had told Khan that – Steven – had the key.

TWENTY-FOUR

Nervous exhaustion made Steven fall asleep in the chair at six a.m. but escape from angst was short-lived as daylight probed his eyelids and he woke after little more than an hour. For one glorious moment he thought he'd been having a bad dream, but reality was quick to assert itself and insist he had to accept all that had happened. He padded through to the bathroom and turned on the shower, waiting for a few moments to let it reach the right temperature before stepping in to let the warm water ease away the annoying crick that had appeared in his neck.

Khan knew he had the key but he and Khan had never met face to face and Khan wouldn't know where he lived. Fortunately, the only information he'd given Liam was his mobile phone number. It wouldn't take Khan long to check out where Sci-Med was located if he didn't already know, but for the moment that was as far as it went . . . unless of course Khan still had credibility in intelligence circles and could seek assistance. It was conceivable that only Steven and Macmillan knew that he was some kind of renegade, but at the moment there was no point of contact between Sci-Med and the usual agencies so there was no way of checking.

Showered, shaved and shampooed, Steven put on a light blue shirt, his Parachute Regiment tie and a dark blue suit. The idea was to look better than he felt. 'Image over substance, Dunbar,' he murmured. 'Way of the world these days.' He made a slight adjustment to the holster under his left arm to ensure that the bulge was as snug a fit as possible and set off for the Home Office.

John Macmillan arrived just after he did and they took coffee through to Macmillan's office, where Steven explained what he now believed Khan was after.

'I see,' said Macmillan slowly. 'Not a happy thought. He has the disk but you have the key. Well, one thing's for sure, the contents must be more important than we imagined.'

Steven nodded. 'You're right, but you can understand how it happened. Simone would have taken the envelope at face value when she came across it. After all, it said vaccination schedules. She would have taken it with her when she left, believing it to be evidence of poor practice by what turned out to be a fake aid agency team. She wanted to bring this to light at the Prague conference, but after the way she was treated she became suspicious and posted the envelope to the North lab in London, first removing the memory card which she sent to me. She probably thought that the card was just a copy of what was on the disk and was making sure that the information wasn't destroyed.'

Macmillan nodded and Steven continued. 'The North lab saw *Vaccination schedules* on the envelope and wouldn't have attached much significance to it either. They'd assume it was just Simone getting her point across about fake aid teams, not very interesting because by that time everyone knew about it.'

'And they wouldn't know about the existence of the memory card just as you didn't know about the disk,' added Macmillan.

'Exactly. And when they did look at it and couldn't make head or tail of it they'd assume it had been damaged in transit, just as I thought about the card.'

'But together they contain information that Khan is willing to kill for. Details of the new bio-weapon?' suggested Macmillan.

Steven made a face. 'Why would that be lying around in a remote mountain village in Afghanistan?'

It was Macmillan's turn to make a face. 'Fair point.'

'Unless it had been left there for someone to pick up?' said Steven. 'Simone and her team just happened to come along at the wrong time – or the right time, depending on how you look at it.'

'I can't see the British or the Americans leaving sensitive information in a place like that, can you?'

'In which case I think it's odds on the information must have
been stolen and the village was being used as an intermediate
staging post. But by whom?'

'Well, it wouldn't be much use to a mountain goatherd,' said
Macmillan. 'I think we're looking at the third element in this dirty
affair: Pakistani intelligence.'

'And that's where Khan comes in. Maybe he was the one who
was supposed to pick up the envelope in the village?' suggested
Steven.

'Hence his killing spree across Europe. He's been trying to get
it back.'

'He must have worked out that Simone had taken the envelope
and questioned her about it at the Prague conference. He must
have spooked her so much that she put it in the post before he
killed her to keep her quiet about what he was after. Then he
went in pursuit of Aline in case Simone had given it to her and
she told him what Simone had done . . . and that must have been
what she was going to tell me over dinner in Paris, only she never
got the chance, the bastard. Then he moved to London to confront
Tom North who gave him the disk but maintained he didn't know
about the card, ditto Dan Hausman, and then finally Liam who
told him . . . that I have it.'

'It all fits, as they say,' said Macmillan.

'Not quite,' said Steven. 'I'm not sure where Bill Andrews and
the CIA fit into all of this unless Andrews has gone rogue too
and the pair of them are planning on selling to the highest bidder.'

'There would probably be considerable demand,' conceded
Macmillan. 'And I take it you still believe Andrews was working
with Khan over the murder of your friend?'

'Everything points to it. He lied when he pretended not to
know Khan when they knew each other very well from way back.
Then he told me Khan had gone back to Afghanistan when, in
fact, he was on his way to Paris.'

'A couple of bad apples,' said Macmillan.

'And they're both in London,' said Steven.

'Where is the memory card?'

'In my desk drawer.'

'Here or at home?'

'Here,' said Steven with a slight smile at Macmillan's obvious priority.

'We'd better ensure its security, if you're agreeable?'

'Agreed.'

'Good,' said Macmillan, exchanging a glance with Steven that acknowledged that each of them knew they were ensuring the location of the card would remain secret even if one or both of them were to be taken and subjected to coercion. If they didn't know, they couldn't tell. It was a bonding moment that few would experience. 'I'll ask Jean to put it in the system.'

As if on cue, Jean Roberts knocked and entered. 'Sir John, the computer people you requested are here.' She turned to Steven. 'Steven, the new mobile phone you asked for is on my desk.'

Steven thanked her. He was destroying that particular link between himself and Khan, especially any chance of GPS tracking it might be possible to instigate on the old phone. He got up to go through to his own office.

Macmillan said, 'I'll brief our consultants in broad terms, remind them they've signed the Official Secrets Act et cetera and then pass them over to you. Let's hope Charlie phones soon with details of where the stuff is and we can get started.'

'I'll go get that card.'

Macmillan had barely finished briefing the two computer experts retained on Sci-Med's consultancy list when the phone call from Charlie Malloy came.

'John, I've really gone out on a limb over this,' said Malloy.

'I know, Charlie, and I really appreciate it.'

'I'm doing the usual police thing of resenting any outside inter- ference in what we see as a straightforward case of murder . . .

even when the "outside interference" is coming from HMG's spooks, if you get my meaning.'

'I can imagine, Charlie.'

'There's a limit to how long I can play the bloody-minded copper before they flush me and my pension down the toilet. I don't really have a good reason for removing all that computer stuff.'

'We'll be as quick as we can. Our computer people are waiting here and Steven is briefing them as we speak.'

'Good. The gear is in a police warehouse at thirty-four Crompton Lane: the entry key is eight-seven-four-one.'

'Got that. We'll be as quick as we can. And Charlie?' Macmillan had a sudden thought.

'Yes?'

'Did you get Steven's request about ballistics on the bullets?'

'Yes. It's being dealt with.'

'It occurs to me that if you were the one to forward the info and request to Inspector Le Grice in Paris and get confirmation, you would have your valid reason for removing computer equipment . . . you suspected an international element to the crime?'

'Christ, John, you're not as dumb as I thought.'

'Good to know, Charlie,' said Macmillan urbanely. 'I'll let Steven know what's happening.'

Steven had almost finished his briefing when Macmillan came in with the news that everything was ready. He waited until Steven had finished.

'To conclude, we have very limited time on site. Anything that can be copied should be copied and brought back here for analysis. We are looking for any kind of correspondence – incoming or outgoing – from Dr Thomas North and Dr Daniel Hausman with special emphasis on anything emanating from Fort Detrick in the USA and Porton Down in England. We suspect the primary versions of these messages will have been wiped but back-ups on the servers might still be there. Any questions?

The two consultants, one a woman in her thirties and the other a male around the same age, both academics, one with expertise in distance learning techniques and the other in communications security, shook their heads.

'Good,' said Macmillan. He turned to Steven and said, 'I've arranged with Lukas Neubauer to meet you there. He'll remain with these good people and deal with any requests they might make for services and equipment.

'Good,' said Steven. 'Let's go.'

TWENTY-FIVE

Lukas Neubauer, section head at Lundborg Analytical, the contract labs that Sci-Med called in for specialist advice and analysis, was waiting outside the premises in Crompton Lane when Steven and the consultants arrived. He and Steven greeted each other warmly, their friendship having been cemented over the course of many investigations in the past. Neubauer was primarily a biologist but was in reality a polymath with a wide knowledge of just about everything. Steven had yet to discover a field that the expatriate Czech did not know a lot about. He had an insatiable thirst for learning.

Steven introduced the two consultants to him and was pleased to see Neubauer's outgoing personality and charm put them at their ease. Anything they needed, they only had to ask . . . including lunch.

Steven and Neubauer exchanged pleasantries while the other two moved into their comfort zone through plugging things in and setting things up.

'How's business at Lundborg?' Steven asked.

'Ticking over,' replied Neubauer. 'People are cutting back on everything these days including contract research so we depend on our regular customers like Sci-Med. I have to admit I was hoping for a big juicy DNA sequencing job when Sir John phoned but . . . baby-sitting's okay.' He and Steven smiled, both knowing what was coming next. Together they intoned, 'Keeps the wolf from the door.'

Steven returned to the Home Office to do what he least liked doing, waiting. There was no question of his being able to settle to anything. Instead he alternated between pacing in his office and looking out of the window, wondering how the day was going to turn out. The first piece of news came just after eleven o'clock, not from Crompton Lane but in the form of a courtesy call from Philippe Le Grice in Paris confirming that the bullets which had killed Hausman and Liam had indeed been fired from the gun used to execute Aline Lagarde.

Steven gave the news to Macmillan, who was pleased to hear something positive for a change. 'Charlie must be relieved,' he said. 'It should help his blood pressure and give him a bit of breathing space.'

'Maybe you should warn him not to use the information unless he really has to,' said Steven. 'We'll need more in the way of direct evidence to nail Khan . . . like finding the gun on him.'

'Or getting a DNA match from either the Paris hotel or the North lab, preferably both,' said Macmillan.

'He's a pro; chances are he wore gloves on both occasions and left nothing behind. But one way or the other . . .'

Macmillan looked at him. 'Don't do anything silly, Steven. You and I haven't exactly made many friends in high places over this business and there are those who will be looking for any excuse. As I've said many times before, the only thing that keeps us in business is Her Majesty's Opposition – regardless of who they are – and the capital they'd make out of any government trying to shut us up.'

'Understood,' said Steven.

The conversation ended when Charlie Malloy phoned to convey news of the pressure he was under and to urge Sci-Med to be as quick as possible. Steven heard Macmillan say, 'Believe me, Charlie, our people are working flat out as we speak. We'll be out of Crompton Lane in no time. I'll let you know the minute it happens.'

Macmillan ended the call and looked at the clock on the wall. 'Think we should phone Lukas?' he asked.

Steven shook his head. 'He knows we're on borrowed time. I told him.'

He noted that Macmillan's behaviour was now mimicking his own earlier as Sir John stopped fidgeting with his pen to get up and go over to look out of the window. 'God, I hope they find something,' he said without turning round. 'If they don't, we really are up that well-known creek without means of propulsion and with half the Royal Navy bearing down on us.'

Steven returned to his own office to fidget and pace on his own.

Lukas Neubauer called at twelve thirty. 'Your people say they've done all they can here. They've copied quite a lot for further analysis and they'd like to hang on to one piece of the confiscated equipment, with your permission?'

Steven only took a moment to decide. 'Yes, that's fine.'

'Good,' said Neubauer. 'I'll bring everything over to the Home Office and then take your people to lunch – on Sci-Med of course. They'll continue their analysis this afternoon.'

'Well done, Lukas. I'll tell John he can let the police know we're finished. I take it there will be no sign left of our activities?'

'Not a trace.'

Macmillan phoned Charlie Malloy. 'We're out of Crompton Lane, Charlie. There's just one small problem . . .'

'What?' asked a nervous Malloy.

'We've hung on to one piece of equipment. The experts weren't finished with it but I told them how anxious you were to have us out of there.'

Steven smiled at the white lie.

Malloy sighed. 'Well, it's not that unusual for bits of confiscated stuff to get mislaid for a while. Thanks, John.'

'No, thank you, Charlie. I owe you.'

'I'll remind you.'

Steven and Macmillan were both suffused with a sense of relief. 'That's one hurdle over,' said Steven.

'Let's hope for a productive afternoon,' said Macmillan.

Steven went out for a sandwich and a walk in the fresh air. This was yet another weekend when he wouldn't manage to get up to Scotland to see his daughter and thoughts about that had finally worked their way to the top of the queue. He'd phone Sue tonight and speak to Jenny for a while, but this thought only made him reflect on how often he'd had to do this in the past. But while feeling bad about it he started to wonder whether he was feeling sorry for Jenny or himself.

The truth was that Jenny was perfectly happy – the last time they'd spoken she'd been bubbling with enthusiasm about her part in a new school play – and Sue and Richard were perfectly content with the situation. It was he who had misgivings and, if he were totally honest, it was because he could sense a distinct feeling of fading away into the background, of not really mattering. Was this the price that had to be paid for the sort of life he led? A failure to form secure and lasting relationships?

There was certainly precedent, he thought, when he considered the 'new lives' of some of his former comrades in Special Forces when they returned to civvy street: the failed attempts to run pubs in the country, the short-lived marriages, the problems involving the police. Maybe it was never truly over. Once you'd walked the tightrope between life and death there was no chance of truly settling down on terra firma. He was lucky; he hadn't had to give up the high wire. Life with Sci-Med had its moments, like knowing that somewhere, not a million miles away from where he was currently standing, someone named Ranjit Khan was coming after him.

Steven returned to the Home Office to hear that the computer people were hard at work upstairs. 'No results as yet,' he was told. 'Are you all right, Steven?' Jean Roberts asked as an afterthought.

'Sure, fine,' he replied.

An hour later, Macmillan looked round his door. 'I've got Scott Jamieson on the phone. He'd like a word with you. I can never transfer these damned calls.'

Steven went through to Macmillan's office while Macmillan chatted outside to Jean.

'Hello, Scott, how are you? Long time no see.'

'Yes, it's been a while. Look, I'll come straight to the point. You know that I took over the ME investigation from you?'

'Yes. How's it going?'

'That's the thing . . . I've caught one of the buggers. He was vandalising a car outside the home of a microbiologist who works on ME.'

'Good for you, old son . . . but isn't that the job of the police?'

'Yes, well, you could say that. Let's say I was alleviating the boredom.'

Steven laughed. He liked Scott Jamieson a lot; he was a good investigator and there was no one he'd rather have beside him in a tight spot. 'Fair enough. What can I do for you?'

'I'd like you to come and see this guy.'

'Are you kidding?' Steven exclaimed. 'I'm up to my neck. I'm on a code red.'

'I know you are,' replied Jamieson calmly. 'I'd still like you to come and see him.'

Steven bit his tongue and read between the lines. There had to be a very good reason for Scott's request, one that he obviously didn't want to reveal over the phone. 'Where are you?'

'Ayton Hill Farm.'

'Where's that?'

'On the North Yorkshire moors.'

Steven had to work hard at stifling his reaction. No, Scott wasn't having a laugh and yes, he did know how bloody far that was from London. That reason must be fucking brilliant. 'Do you have a grid reference?'

Jamieson read it out and Steven hung up.

'Everything all right?' asked Macmillan as Steven rushed past on the way to his own office.

'Tell you later.' Steven closed the door behind him and called the internal number of the duty officer assigned to his code red status. 'I need a helicopter. City Airport to North Yorkshire. Fast as you like.'

'Understood. I'll call you.'

Steven smiled. That was the way things worked under code red. No questions, no form filling, no explanations until the code red was over.

The duty man called back in under five minutes. 'It'll be on the tarmac in fifteen minutes.'

TWENTY-SIX

'Are they expecting us?' asked the pilot.

'Sorry, don't know,' replied Steven, looking down at the bleak moorland farm below.

'Place looks deserted . . . no signs of life, and thankfully not much in the way of power lines . . . just one on the northern boundary as far as I can see, but I'd appreciate if you'd keep your eyes peeled.'

The helicopter banked sharply to the left as the pilot began a circle of the farm below, looking for possible problems on the ground. 'Don't want to put her down in a bloody bog.'

He opted for a piece of flat ground to the right of a large barn next to the main farmhouse building. Still no one had emerged from inside, making Steven feel anxious. He thought Scott Jamieson might have come out to welcome them with a wave or to point to a suitable landing spot, but of course Jamieson didn't know how or when he was coming.

The helicopter settled gently on the grass, the pilot ready to gun the engine at the first sign of any instability in the ground, but it seemed firm enough. He kept the rotor blades turning while Steven decided on the best way of approaching the building. He made his decision and told the pilot to keep the engines running until he gave him a signal that all was well. Then he removed his helmet and released himself from his seat harness and communications wiring before opening the door and dropping to the ground.

His plan was to sprint into the lee of the barn and approach the house using the barn as cover, not because of any belief that he was in danger, more a case of old habits dying hard. The plan was made redundant when the farmhouse door opened and Scott Jamieson appeared with a smile on his face and a pistol in his hand which he was now dangling by his side.

Steven signalled to the pilot to cut the engines and the beat of the rotors faded as he walked over to the house.

'I wasn't sure it was you,' explained Scott.

'I thought that might be the case. What's with the weapon?'

'I confiscated it from him indoors. I thought the copter might be full of his pals.'

'The vandal?' asked Steven, surprised.

'Yep. He says he knows you.'

Steven's face registered disbelief as he was led indoors and into a room where a man was secured to a chair with rope bindings. 'We appear to have a conflict of interests,' Jamieson announced.

Steven couldn't believe his eyes. 'Ricksen!' he exclaimed.

'Then you two do know each other,' said Scott. 'He wouldn't tell me anything, said he'd only speak to you. I saw him slashing the tyres of a car belonging to a research microbiologist who lives about twenty miles from here so I tailed him, hoping he'd lead me to the organisers of the Popular Front for the Liberation of ME Sufferers. Instead I end up holding an MI5 officer in one of their own safe houses. I was going to ask John what the hell I should do with him but chummy here kept insisting he knew you and you'd want to hear his side of things.'

'Wow,' said Steven. 'I think we can do away with the bindings. How are you, John?'

'I've had better days,' replied Ricksen, appearing more than a little crestfallen.

'Has Five been behind all the attacks on ME researchers?'

Ricksen nodded, adding, 'Christ, what a mess.'

'It'll make a cracking story for the *Sun*,' said Jamieson.

'D notices will fall like confetti,' snapped Ricksen.

'So what's it all about, John?' asked Steven. 'And what's the mess you're now in to do with me?

171

'C'mon, Steven, we've known each other a long time,' said Ricksen. 'We've even looked out for each other on occasion. Okay, there's a bit of rivalry between Five and Sci-Med, but when push comes to shove we know we can call on each other for a bit of help.'

Steven nodded. 'True,' he conceded, 'but everyone's been snubbing Sci-Med lately and this is quite a hole you've dug for yourself . . . and Five. I'm getting dizzy just looking down into it.'

'Look, there's a lot of strange stuff going on. I hoped we might come to an arrangement . . . exchange what we know . . . pool our resources?'

Steven and Jamieson exchanged doubtful glances.

'There's a big secret . . .' said Ricksen, immediately capturing Steven's attention.

'Go on.'

'That's the thing. Only people at the very top know what it is and they are going to enormous lengths to keep it that way. The Americans are involved and I get the impression that Pakistani intelligence are in the mix too.'

'They are,' said Steven. 'One of their agents, a guy called Ranjit Khan, has gone rogue. He's killed five people so far, trying to get his hands on this secret. He killed my friend Simone Ricard, and it was him who was responsible for Dr North's death, and the two last night.'

'Shit, we knew Khan was in the country. We thought he was working with Six.'

'So presumably does MI6,' said Steven. 'Apparently he's decided to become self-employed: he wants the secret for himself.'

'That's worth knowing.'

'Perhaps you'll return the favour. Why have you been targeting ME researchers?'

'HMG wants research on ME to stop but no one's saying why. It's connected to this damned secret. Our brief is to do what we can to stop current research on ME and discourage anyone from entering the field.'

'By pushing them under a bus?' said Jamieson.

'I swear to God that was just a terrible accident; it was never meant to happen. He was just meant to appear foolish.'

'And he ends up appearing dead,' said Jamieson.

'Christ, I don't like it any more than you guys.'

'Yeah, shit happens,' said Jamieson without a trace of sympathy.

'This is getting us nowhere,' Steven interrupted. 'Okay, cards on the table. We've been thinking along the lines of Porton and the Americans developing a new bio-weapon and testing it illegally on the border between Pakistan and Afghanistan. The Americans have already been caught out putting fake aid teams into the region to help in their hunt for Bin Laden, but there's definitely more to it than that.'

Ricksen seemed taken aback and Steven thought it seemed genuine. 'We knew about the fake team that got DNA evidence proving Bin Laden was in the compound at Abbottabad, but the rest is news to me.'

'There has to be a link between a new bio-weapon and the government stopping research on ME,' said Jamieson.

'If HMG want to stop research on ME, it suggests they already know what causes it,' said Steven.

'And they're developing it as a new weapon,' Ricksen added.

All three thought about this for a few moments.

Steven shook his head. 'Sounds all wrong,' he murmured.

'I agree,' said Jamieson. 'If scientists had discovered the cause of ME they wouldn't have kept it secret – even if it was a government lab that made the breakthrough. They would have taken the enormous credit on offer and set about finding a cure. None of that would have prevented them from developing their discovery as a weapon in the usual way in the usual places if they'd wanted to. There would have been no need for a huge cloak of secrecy. Steven's right; it sounds all wrong.'

'Doesn't sound like much of a weapon either,' said Ricksen. 'Oh, I can't fight today 'cause I'm just too tired . . .'

Steven ignored the sneer and asked, 'So where does that leave us, gentlemen?'

'We still don't know the secret,' said Jamieson.

No one disagreed.

'There is one more thing you should know,' said Ricksen, looking at Steven. 'Two days ago, someone put in a request to see your file.'

'What file?' asked Steven.

'Ours . . . on you.'

Steven took a few moments to digest this before murmuring, 'Just one big happy family, aren't we. Who wanted it?'

'A CIA guy, Bill Andrews.'

'And you just gave him it?'

'Personally, I didn't give him anything,' said Ricksen defensively. 'I just pricked up my ears when I heard your name come up, although it has to be said you're not exactly in the running for employee of the month right now in the corridors of power. You're being seen as a bit of a thorn in the side, if not a complete pain in another part of the anatomy . . .'

'It was ever thus,' joked Jamieson. 'He's mad, bad and dangerous to know.'

Steven was in no mood for humour. The hollow feeling in the pit of his stomach at hearing that his file had been given to Andrews was not going to go away.

'What are we going to do about him?' Jamieson asked with a nod in Ricksen's direction.

'Did you get photographic evidence of him vandalising the car?' asked Steven.

'Certainly did.'

Ricksen looked anxious. 'Oh, come on, guys. You're not going to hang me out to dry . . .'

'Maybe another couple of him standing in the doorway of an MI5 safe house?' suggested Steven. 'And your investigation will have reached a satisfactory conclusion.'

'Sounds good to me,' said Jamieson.

'You can't be serious about giving this to the papers?' said Ricksen, coming close to pleading.

Steven decided the man had had enough. 'Of course not,' he said. 'But you make sure to tell your boss that Sci-Med knows who's been behind the ME attacks and has proof should they need to use it.'

'Understood,' said Ricksen, relieved that the prospect of becoming national news had receded but not looking forward to explaining his capture to his superiors.

'And open season should be declared on Ranjit Khan forthwith. He's not a colleague; he's a dangerous psycho.'

'How about Andrews, the guy who pulled your file?'

'For the moment, the jury's out.'

'Thanks, Steven.'

'Don't mention it. After all . . . we're all on the same side,' said Steven, looking towards Jamieson to share a grin. 'Time to go home, chaps.'

Steven ran towards the helicopter, making circular motions with a raised finger. The engines started as he climbed on board. 'City Airport, James, and don't spare the rotors.'

TWENTY-SEVEN

It was six thirty p.m. when Steven got back to the Home Office, the last twenty minutes having been spent in London's evening rush-hour traffic. He was pleased to find John Macmillan still there, deep in conversation with the two computer experts. 'Ah, there you are,' said Macmillan when Steven knocked and entered. 'Productive day?'

The expression on Macmillan's face suggested he knew about the helicopter requisition. 'Very,' Steven replied confidently. 'How about you folk?'

Macmillan adopted an expression that suggested his ace had just been trumped by a partner in a card game. 'We're not quite there yet but we've been making good progress. Louis and Elspeth have identified correspondence between Dr Hausman and Fort Detrick and between Dr North and . . . the Prime Minister, no less.'

'I'm impressed,' said Steven. 'Well done.'

The computer experts smiled in the self-deprecating way that academics did when being interviewed by the media about their latest discovery. He half expected one of them to say, 'Of course, more work needs to be done.'

'We've still got a bit to do,' said Louis Henderson.

'Mmm,' agreed Elspeth Fiddes. 'We've identified several messages with the criteria you specified and we've traced their paths but what we haven't managed to do is decipher the contents as yet, although we definitely think it possible with suitable techniques. Another day perhaps.'

'Maybe two,' cautioned Henderson, making Steven wonder unkindly what their daily rate was.

'They've uncovered more than one reference to something called "the discovery",' Macmillan interjected.

'Sounds promising,' said Steven. 'In fact, it sounds exactly what we're looking for.'

Macmillan smiled. 'These good people are now going to take a break before continuing into the evening. Jean has arranged for food to be brought in. Their families have been very understanding.'

'We're all very grateful to you,' said Steven. 'This really is important.'

Jean Roberts, who had also stayed behind to organise the ordering and delivery of take-away meals for the experts, announced that the food had arrived. Macmillan thanked her and ushered Fiddes and Henderson out of his office and into Jean's care with more thanks. He closed the door behind them. 'Now, about this helicopter charter business?'

Steven explained about the request from Scott Jamieson and all that had transpired from his flight to Yorkshire. 'In effect, we have a successful completion to Scott's investigation. We know exactly who's been behind the ME attacks all along – although we're not sure why – and MI5 remains in our debt as long as we care to keep our mouths shut about their involvement. I also suggested to Ricksen that Khan be blown away on sight.'

'Not sure that's a term HMG would be too keen on,' said Macmillan.

'Eliminated with extreme prejudice if you prefer, sir – with the appropriate paperwork in place, of course . . . duly signed by a defence minister, the Bishop of London and Coco the Clown.'

'Don't push it, Dunbar. Do you realise how much a helicopter costs per hour?'

Steven smiled and so did Macmillan after a moment. 'Bloody well done,' he said. 'Look, I'm going to stay on here until the computer people call it a night, so why don't you go home? I'll call if they come up with anything.'

'Thanks,' said Steven. 'That's good of you.'

'Not entirely altruistic,' said Macmillan. 'Lady Macmillan is having her pals round to play bridge this evening. I'm better off here. I might knock over the cauldron.'

Steven set off home to Marlborough Court. It had been a long day and the noise of helicopter rotor blades still seemed to be beating somewhere inside his head. His plan was to run a hot bath, take a drink through with him and settle back in the suds before calling Sue on the mobile. He'd have to keep his other mobile – the Sci-Med BlackBerry – beside him in case of any developments at the Home Office but, with a bit of luck, he might have a decent soak and time to unwind after a day that had seen him sprint from the heart of London to the Yorkshire moors and back again. The only thing militating against this at the moment was the fact that he was being followed.

It had started as a suspicion – a casual sideways glance when crossing a road had picked up a male figure about thirty metres behind, nothing that warranted a second thought until the same figure registered in the same position at the next crossing. This time it did merit a second thought and a third and a fourth. All thoughts of a relaxing evening vanished in an instant to be replaced by nerve-tingling awareness.

He quickened his pace for the next two hundred metres and then, as he spotted a litter bin up ahead, he pulled out a tissue from his pocket and pretended to blow his nose. As he reached the bin, he paused and turned slightly to drop the tissue inside – just enough to confirm that his tail was still about thirty metres back. He had quickened his pace too.

Khan couldn't afford to kill him: he needed him alive to have any hope of getting his hands on the key that meant so much. Apart from that, the streets were too busy to pull a gun out and hope to remain unnoticed. He too was inhibited: opening fire on a busy London street was not an option. Steven decided to force the issue. He changed his route and turned down a dark lane leading to the river. The lane was home to the premises of a van hire company whose vans he knew would be parked on both sides of the lane as their yard was too small to house their entire fleet – something that the neighbouring businesses continually complained about but tonight was exactly what Steven was counting on. Khan wouldn't realise it but he was no longer the hunter; he'd just become the hunted.

Steven stepped off the kerb as if to cross between two of the white vans, knowing that he would be out of sight until Khan picked him up again on the other side – only he didn't cross. He remained between the two vans and counted to five before returning to the same side where he ran back fifteen metres or so before dodging between another two vans and standing still. Khan, not seeing him on the other side, would return to this one. Steven crossed and ran back another few metres before doing the same again. He repeated the manoeuvre until he was sure he was behind Khan.

Steven sneaked a look from behind one of the vans and saw Khan standing in the middle of the lane, looking towards the end as if puzzled. He looked up at the buildings on either side as if wondering which one his quarry had gone into but they were all in darkness. Steven read his mind: Khan would have to assume it was a lost cause and turn back.

Steven withdrew his pistol and waited between the two vans for Khan to pass by. As he did so, Steven levelled the Glock and said, 'Psst.'

Khan froze in his tracks then turned slowly to have the ambient light reveal that he wasn't Khan at all. It was Bill Andrews.

Andrews took in the gun and said, 'Steven, buddy, what the hell?'

'Remove your weapon and place it slowly on the ground.'

'What the hell is this?'

'Do it.'

Andrews did what he was told, still protesting, 'Steven, come on, man, we're on the same side.'

'Now step back.' Steven picked up the weapon and put it in

179

his pocket. 'Now start walking down the lane. I'll be right behind you.'

When they reached the junction at the end, Steven ordered Andrews to cross the road and start descending the old stone steps he'd find on the other side. They led down to the Thames which, at half-tide, was lapping over the green slime on the bottom three or four steps.

Andrews could now see that there was no destination ahead other than the sluggish river and panic appeared in his voice – albeit controlled panic. 'What the hell are you doing, man? What are we doing here?'

'Justice for Simone,' said Steven. 'Time to pay for what you did to my friend.'

'This is crazy,' exclaimed Andrews. 'I had nothing to do with that, Steven. As God is my witness I believed it was an accident until last week when I found out about Ranjit Khan. That's why I was following you; I came to warn you about Khan.'

'Sure you did. You pretended not to know Khan when I spoke to you in Paris when in fact you and he had been buddies for years. You even played houses when you were at Harvard together.'

'Sure we did, but come on, man, he was Pakistani intelligence and I – as I suppose you now know – am CIA. We didn't want to advertise any intelligence interests at the time.'

'You told me he'd returned to Pakistan when in fact he flew to Paris where he killed Aline Lagarde.'

'Christ, man, I thought he *had* returned to Pakistan. I genuinely thought that. I didn't know the bastard had a different agenda. That's what I came to warn you about.'

'You and Khan killed Simone. You were working together.'

'No,' insisted Andrews, 'you've got it all wrong. It was just like I told you; I lost my contact lens and made a stupid joke about it. The next thing I knew was that Simone was over the balcony.'

'Khan put her over . . . while you created a diversion.'

'Look, it didn't occur to me at the time that Khan had anything to do with it. I didn't know he had any reason to, but in the light

180

of what I've learned recently . . . it might well be true. But I swear to God, I personally had nothing to do with it.'

The water level had risen so that the Thames was now lapping over Andrews' shoes. He seemed not to notice as he looked pleadingly at Steven.

'Remove one of your contact lenses,' said Steven.

'What?'

'You heard. I don't think you wear contact lenses. If you do, I just might believe you. If you don't, it was a diversion in Prague and it's kiss-your-arse-goodbye time.'

Andrews seemed to freeze completely for a few seconds: Steven suspected that he must be contemplating one last desperate move to save his skin. He moved the Glock slightly to emphasise that he was entirely focused on the matter in hand and could pull the trigger faster than Andrews could mount any last-ditch attack. 'I'm waiting.'

Andrews put his hands to his face and went through the motions of removing a contact lens. Steven remained suspicious, thinking that this was exactly what he'd do in Andrews' position before going for a last-minute lunge.

'There you go,' said Andrews, holding out his right hand, palm upwards.

It was too dark for Steven to see. 'Turn around: put your hand behind your back and then open it.'

Andrews complied, the water now sloshing round his ankles.

Steven moved down two steps and pressed the barrel of his gun against the back of Andrews' neck. 'Don't move a muscle,' he warned. He looked down and saw the lens sitting in Andrews' palm. He removed it with the tip of his index finger then replaced it. 'You live to fight another day.'

TWENTY-EIGHT

Steven replaced the Glock in its holster and took out Andrews' gun from his pocket. He removed the magazine and threw the clip in the river before handing the weapon back to Andrews. 'You're not out of the woods yet.'

'What happens now? Where are we going?' asked Andrews at the top of the steps.

'My place.'

When Andrews was sitting at his kitchen table, his socks and shoes drying on a radiator, Steven put a mug of coffee down in front of him and said, 'Now, tell me everything.'

'Only a few at the very top know everything,' said Andrews ruefully.

Steven didn't feel inclined to argue. 'Then tell me what you do know. Tell me why my friend and four other people have been murdered and tell me exactly what your lot and mine have been up to in Afghanistan.'

'As I understand it, we've been trying out an agent developed at Fort Detrick on remote populations in the Khyber Pakhtunkhwa. I know it sounds awful but I'm told it was absolutely essential to carry out this work in the national interest of our countries.'

'Why?'

Andrews grew uncomfortable. 'I don't rightly know.'

This elicited a cold, blank stare from Steven.

'I really don't. To be honest, the agent didn't appear to make people that sick but I was told that there was to be more than one stage to the operation. Fort Detrick and your Porton Down were preparing the next stages.'

'Go on.'

'Your friend Simone and her team came across one of the villages by accident. I don't think she realised what was going on but she was pretty upset about the children's vaccination schedules and wanted to complain about that. It was no big deal for us. By that time all the right people had been told about the CIA teams looking for Bin Laden.'

'So why kill her?'

Andrews swallowed nervously. 'I swear to God, man, I don't know. I had nothing to do with it.'

'But?'

'Presumably, Simone knew more than she let on, or maybe she got hold of something that really pissed somebody off.'

'Like Khan.'

'I guess. We thought Khan was with us but it turns out that he is part of a Pakistani faction that has plans for taking on India in a big way. The old enemy.'

'How did you reach that conclusion?'

'My boss told me something had gone badly wrong. The guys at Fort Detrick were ready with the final stage of the experiment, or whatever you want to call it. One of their top scientists was sent out to a top-level meeting in Pakistan with a CIA-led team. The guy was supposed to bring our allies up to speed but they never made it. They set off from Islamabad one morning with a guide from Pakistani intelligence and disappeared off the face of the planet. We think the guide set them up.'

'So the information fell into the wrong hands?'

'We thought not. The agency didn't trust Pakistani intelligence. They had a plan B in place if there was any kind of double-cross. It was deployed when our guy didn't call in by a certain time and we thought the info had been destroyed along with the punks who ambushed our guys, but new intelligence says not. Khan's behaviour suggests it's still out there somewhere.'

Steven didn't tell Andrews what it was or where. 'But presumably Fort Detrick still has all the details?'

'Oh, sure. It's just a question of them not wanting the info to fall into the wrong hands.'

'Or any hands other than theirs,' said Steven.

Andrews shrugged. 'Hey, maybe that's what Simone discovered?'

'Maybe.'

'So where do we go from here?'

'I take it you're taking steps to deal with Khan, now he's no longer one of your pals?'

Andrews looked uncomfortable again. 'Khan's crimes are seen as a European affair. We don't like to . . . interfere in the internal affairs of our allies.'

'Isn't that just the sweetest thing?' said Steven.

Andrews looked down at the table top. 'What do you intend to do now?' he asked.

Steven shook his head. 'Just go,' he said. 'Just go.'

Nothing more was said as Steven waited for Andrews to put his socks and shoes on before showing him the door. He opened the kitchen window to let out the lingering odour of Thames-soaked footwear before closing the door behind him and going through to the lounge where he poured himself a drink.

'Jesus,' he muttered as he started to assess what he'd learned from the encounter with Andrews. Not a lot, was his conclusion, although it was nice to have what he'd already worked out confirmed. The British, US and Pakistani governments had colluded over the testing of a new bio-agent on people on the North West Frontier – or whatever they called it now. If that was good enough for Kipling it would do for him, he thought, feeling bolshie about the whole business. Andrews had said that carrying out the experiment was of the utmost importance to the security of both their countries although he didn't know why. That, Steven concluded, was still a secret – the secret known by the few.

He'd had enough for one day; it was too late to speak to Jenny, so he called Tally. He didn't want to tell her anything about his day; he just wanted to hear her voice.

Macmillan called just after ten when Steven, feeling better after talking to Tally, was watching the news on TV. He killed the sound and listened expectantly.

'The computer people have recovered the content of a letter sent from the Prime Minister's office to Tom North. It impresses on North that what they call "the discovery" must remain secret at all costs until such time as Porton or Fort Detrick have come up with a way of dealing with what they term "the problem". Make any sense?'

After considering for a few moments, Steven said not.

'I'm going to tell the computer people to go home and get some rest,' said Macmillan. 'They've done well, and with a bit of luck they'll come up with more tomorrow.'

'I was going to leave off telling you this until tomorrow,' said Steven, 'but, as you've called, I had a bit of a run-in with Bill Andrews of the CIA earlier on . . .'

He heard the short intake of breath at the other end of the phone which translated in his mind into 'All I need'. 'I caught him following me. He insists he was going to warn me about Khan's having gone rogue. After a bit of a chat, I think I believe him. He says Khan is part of some militant anti-India faction but he doesn't know what he's after.'

'Did you tell him?'

'No.'

'Did you ask him about the secret?'

'He doesn't know any more than we do.'

'Pity. Still, let's hope for a more productive day tomorrow.'

Steven went through to the kitchen and closed the window; all traces of his earlier guest had now gone. He felt hungry but, as he hadn't been to the supermarket for some time, wasn't quite sure what he had in store.

The fridge revealed some bacon with a slightly greenish sheen to it when held at an angle and a small slab of Cheddar cheese on which Sir Alexander Fleming might have been able to make a significant discovery in another era. The lettuce looked as if the US Air Force had attacked it with Agent Orange and the duck pâté might have served well in the pointing of brickwork. The cupboard above the fridge, however, yielded a large tin of corned beef and a small one of baked beans, which gave his morale a boost and prompted him to murmur, 'And a Michelin star goes to . . . Steven Dunbar.'

As always, after a day in which a lot had happened, Steven was finding it difficult to unwind. His earlier plan to have a long soak had of course been scuppered by the encounter with Andrews. That had sent his adrenalin levels soaring and it was taking a long time for them to subside. He was no longer hungry; he didn't want any more to drink; he didn't want to watch TV but he knew if he went to bed he wouldn't sleep. He seemed destined to continue fidgeting until he realised there was a way he could speed the unwinding process up. He checked the weather outside from the window before changing into a track suit and trainers. It was eleven o'clock but he was going out for a run. He would run until exhaustion freed him from restlessness.

An hour later he arrived back at Marlborough Court thinking he might have overdone it. Sweat dripped from his face on to the floor of the lift and he experienced the slight feeling of nausea that athletes encountered when pushing themselves to the limit. It passed without incident, however, and was replaced by a pleasant endorphin rush once he had showered and settled down with a cold Peroni beer. He was enjoying a warm feeling of well-being when the phone rang.

'Dr Dunbar?'

'Who is this?'

'Perhaps you'd like three guesses, doctor?'

The cultured voice and Pakistani accent made Steven's blood run cold. He was talking to Simone's killer.

'You have something I want, doctor, and I would be grateful if you would deliver it to me.'

Alarm bells were ringing in Steven's head. Khan sounded too sure of himself, like a man about to show a hand of four aces. 'What are you talking about?'

'Forget the nonsense, please. There isn't time, as you are about to appreciate. I want the memory card or the next time you see your daughter will be at her funeral.'

'What?' exclaimed Steven, feeling sick to his stomach. 'My daughter? What the hell are you talking about?'

Steven stopped when a familiar voice came on the line. 'Daddy, Daddy, there's a bad man in the house . . .'

'Jenny?'

Khan was back on the line. 'I don't have to warn you about involving outside agencies. That goes without saying. Start by flying into Edinburgh Airport with the card. Be there by noon and await my instructions.'

TWENTY-NINE

Steven was beside himself. Khan had got inside the house at Glenvane and was holding Jenny hostage. Right now it didn't matter where he had obtained the information. What mattered was that he was holding his daughter and was demanding the memory card in exchange for her life – a card he no longer had. In what now seemed like some hellish irony, he had handed it over to be held under secure conditions to stop it falling into the wrong hands.

There had to be a way round this. He would get in touch with Jean Roberts who had put the card into safe keeping. He would explain what had happened and she would . . . no, she wouldn't. She couldn't. That's not how the system worked. Having worked out that the card was the thing Khan was after in his murderous rampage, he and Macmillan had agreed that it be put into the government's security system, which would keep it safe in the event of any kind of coercion or blackmail attempt being applied to individuals. Nothing he or Macmillan said would make any difference now. HMG did not pay ransoms, give in to blackmail or make deals with criminals. Steven was in the very position the system was designed to guard against.

He felt as if he were being crucified slowly, one nail at a time. Every idea he came up with seemed to end in a negative. He found himself fighting his way through successive waves of fear and anger which overwhelmed his ability to think clearly. Experience insisted on reminding him that these emotions were his enemy. However difficult it was, he must calm down. He must accept that he couldn't get his hands on the card: there was just no way to do it, therefore there was no point in considering it further. He had to save Jenny by other means. What other means?

There was no point in waking Macmillan. They would just end up going over the same ground and time was of the essence. Calling up the police in Scotland was also a non-starter and would almost certainly lead to disaster. Explanations would be required, referrals, approvals, permissions and God knows what before anyone actually did anything. There wasn't time.

He would fly into Edinburgh as instructed. He would follow further instructions to the letter and would hand over a memory card. It couldn't be the card that Khan wanted so that's when the big bluff would begin. There was no way of knowing how much time there would be before the deception was discovered but that, he acknowledged with a chill running down his spine, might well be irrelevant. On past performance, there would be no trade. Khan would accept the card and kill both him and Jenny. To give Jenny any chance at all against the bastard he would need help, the kind of help that could only come from one place.

It wouldn't be the first time Steven had called on the SAS, known universally as the Regiment, for help, but never before for personal reasons. Ironically, the last time had been to hitch a lift into Afghanistan to visit a field hospital in the course of an investigation. It wasn't something he would do lightly, but Jenny's life was at stake and there was nothing on earth he wouldn't do to save her.

At this late stage there was no official way he could request army involvement. It would have to be a personal appeal. He would be relying on something front line soldiers knew but tended not to broadcast widely. When the chips were down, it wasn't Queen and country they fought for and it wasn't defence of the realm that was uppermost in their minds; they fought for each other. Simple as that.

The rest of it was high-sounding baloney, spouted by politicians as justification for pursuing goals that were becoming increasingly difficult to determine. The Regiment didn't do bullshit. They didn't march through towns with fixed bayonets; they didn't have a royal in a soldier suit as their colonel-in-chief, they didn't accept the freedom to shit in the street, as one wag put it. They didn't need the image. They were the real deal.

Front line camaraderie forged a bond that survived long afterwards. It was the only card he had left to play. He called a number that had been engraved on his memory for years.

'No promises but I'll get back to you,' was the response when he'd finished making his appeal.

The minutes passed like proverbial hours with Steven itching to be doing something, not hanging around waiting. He knew he should be planning what to do if the answer from Hereford was no. He knew he should be . . . telling Tally what had happened. This brought on an extra frisson of anxiety. Tally had been right all along about his job. Normal people did not live like this.

The house phone rang and Steven snatched at it. It was Sue in Scotland.

'He said not to phone the police,' she said, her voice betraying the nightmare she was going through.

'I know, I know,' Steven soothed, making a supreme effort to keep his voice level. 'We have to be strong; we have to keep calm. Tell me what happened.'

He heard Sue swallow in preparation. 'I thought I heard a noise downstairs. I woke Richard and he said it was the wind. Then we both heard it and Richard went downstairs. There was a man with a gun in his hand, an Asian man: he'd broken in. He made Richard call me downstairs and then . . . he hit Richard with the gun and knocked him out cold. He told me to go wake Jenny and bring her down or he'd shoot Richard . . . Poor love, she was terrified.'

Steven closed his eyes and heard Sue sob before regaining control and continuing. 'The next bit you know. He phoned you and made Jenny speak to you. When he'd finished, he said that no one was going to get hurt. He told Jenny that she would see her daddy later but she had to go with him . . . She clung to me . . .

Oh, God, I feel as if I betrayed her . . . He told me to make coffee for him and hot milk for Jenny, then he put something in the milk. When I tried to stop him, he pointed the gun at Richard on the floor and I shut up. He said it was just something to calm her down. After ten minutes or so, when she grew sleepy, he left, taking her with him. Oh, God, this can't be happening.' Sue lost her struggle to maintain composure and broke down.

Steven tried his best to reassure her that things would work out. He'd give Khan what he wanted and Jenny would be back home safe and sound. In reality he wasn't sure whether he believed what he was saying or was writing a letter to Santa Claus. He checked with Sue that she hadn't called the police. She hadn't. 'How's Richard?'

'A nasty gash and a sore head but apart from that I think he's okay. I don't know what we're going to tell the children . . .'

'Hang in there, Sue. Put all your lives on hold for the day. Keep the kids off school. Don't answer the door. Don't talk to anyone. As far as the world's concerned, you've all got flu.'

'I feel so helpless,' sobbed Sue. 'We both do. A man just walked into our house and took away our . . .'

'None of this is your fault,' Steven assured her, wishing that the same could be said for him but knowing it couldn't. It *was* all his fault. 'We have to be practical; we have to stay strong for Jenny's sake.'

Steven's mobile rang and he had to end the call.

'It's an affirmative. Get yourself up to Hereford. When challenged, show your ID and tell them you're with Blue Ranger 7.'

Steven's Porsche could not travel faster than a speeding bullet but he coaxed it into doing its best as it ate up the miles between London and Hereford. Weather conditions were good and traffic at that time in the morning was light. The anticipated appearance of a police traffic patrol at some point did not materialise so there was no need to waste time showing ID and verifying his code red status. The journey was completed without incident.

The mention of Blue Ranger 7 at the gate resulted in his

being shown into a small briefing room in a ground floor suite of three or four rooms where four men sat drinking coffee from mugs with cartoon characters on them, two on chairs and two perched on the edge of a table. Each wore civilian clothes and introduced himself by a single name: Nick, Lenny, Sparks and Stratocaster.

'As in the guitar?' asked Steven of the last one.

The man nodded with a smile but gave no explanation and Steven didn't inquire further. You didn't.

'This never happened, Steven,' said the one named Nick. 'We're about to go off piste as far as them upstairs are concerned.'

'I thought as much,' said Steven, having known full well that any action had to be unofficial. 'Thank you.' The words sounded painfully inadequate but the fact that they came from the heart prompted an acknowledgement of nods all round.

'To business,' said Nick. 'I take it he hasn't been in touch again?'

Steven said not.

'So all we know is that you have to be at Edinburgh Airport by noon?'

Steven nodded.

'So he might be there or he might phone you there with instructions. Did you bring the photo?'

Steven handed over the photograph of Khan Jean had come up with when investigating the participants at the Prague meeting. 'Here you go. Dr Ranjit Khan, Pakistani intelligence . . . but no longer. He's gone private and he's no mug.'

'Good to know,' said Nick. 'Right, let's talk communications: we'll fit you up with some gear and we'll sat-tag you in case you lose the wires early. We'll do it twice just in case he's content with finding one on you if there's a search, but we're all going to have to play this very much by ear. We don't even know if he's doing this on his own, do we?'

'My gut feeling is that it's a solo effort, but no guarantees.'

'Something to bear in mind,' said Nick. 'We'll travel up separately, you by air from Birmingham so you arrive off a scheduled flight just in case he or anyone else is watching. We'll travel up by road . . . with our gear. Are you carrying?'

Steven said not. The prospect of having to go through flight security at some point had made him leave the Glock at home.

Nick handed Steven a small vial of pills. 'To help you stay awake.'

Two of the soldiers left the room to load and check over their vehicle, a Land Rover Defender, while Steven showered and changed into the suit he'd brought with him. He removed the memory card he was going to use from his briefcase and slipped it into the inside pocket of his jacket, pausing briefly to reflect on the enormity of the bluff he was planning. It had been decided that they would all leave at the same time, the soldiers heading directly to Scotland and he to Birmingham Airport. If he had time he would call Tally and tell her what was going on. He deliberately kept his speed down on the motorway in order to concentrate on what he was going to say, but as he entered the car park at the airport he still wasn't sure.

There was no escaping the fact that the next few hours were going to change everything in his life regardless of the outcome. If the worst should happen to Jenny and he should survive, he knew that he would slip all the anchors he had in society. He would walk away from his job, his relationship, his friends, and single-mindedly hunt down Khan and kill him . . . or die in the attempt. There would be no waiting for the wheels of justice to turn. He wasn't civilised to the degree required to lift him above seeking revenge. That's just the way it was.

If, please God, Jenny were to come out of this unscathed in the physical sense there would still be the question of how she would cope mentally. True, she was a child and children were remarkably resilient, but the question must be how deep would the scars run? Sue and Richard too would be traumatised and it was impossible to think that things could ever be the same again between them all. As for Tally . . . he was just about to find out whether their relationship could survive the latest challenge.

THIRTY

Steven bought a ticket on the mid-morning flight to Edinburgh. He bought black coffee and found a quiet spot in the airport lounge where he settled by a window to look out at the grey morning light before calling Tally.

'Steven? I'm glad you called: you sounded a bit distracted last night. I was worried.'

'I'm sorry . . . rather a lot's been happening.'

'Something's the matter,' said Tally, alarmed at the nuance she was picking up in Steven's voice.

'I don't know how Khan found out about Jenny and where she lived but he did. He's kidnapped her and wants to trade her for the memory card Simone enclosed with her letter. Right now I'm at Birmingham Airport waiting to go up to Edinburgh . . . to await his instructions.'

'Oh, my God, Steven . . . Oh, Steven, this is awful . . . poor little love . . . Oh, God, is there anything I can do? Anything at all?'

'No, it's up to me right now,' said Steven. 'I . . . just thought you should know what's going on . . .'

There was a pause before Tally said quietly, 'Of course I should know what's going on; we love each other, don't we? Jenny's part of us, as in the two of us, isn't she?'

'Sorry, I put it badly. I'm not thinking straight. Of course she is. It's just that . . . I suppose I've suddenly become very conscious of just how much my job affects the people around me, the people I love. You were much more aware of it than me. You spelt it out for me more than once and I kept pushing it to the back of my mind.'

'Stop it, Steven,' said Tally, but not unkindly. 'What I said in the past was based on my own selfishness. I thought I had a right to demand a safe and secure life and you should comply with that and fall into line, but I was wrong, and I remember all the unhappiness you went through for me before I insisted you went back to Sci-Med. You're a special person doing a special job, a job that needs doing, and it's the rest of us who should fall into line. Every wife of every soldier serving in Afghanistan has to do this. I've come to realise there's a great army of unsung heroines out there who go through hell every day but accept it without complaint. I'm now one of them. I love you; I'll always be there for you and so will all the people you love, so stop talking nonsense and go get Jenny back.'

Steven managed a smile for the first time in a while. 'Will do.'

The flight north only served to increase Steven's anxiety. He'd never been fond of the enforced proximity to strangers that air travel imposed but today it was the sheer normality of his fellow passengers' behaviour that seemed to get to him; the very things that would normally confer anonymity on people were today doing the opposite. Filling in crossword puzzles, tapping laptop keys, reading newspapers, even the sipping of coffee seemed to imply a complete disregard for the personal agony he was going through.

The seatbelt sign went on as the aircraft crossed over the Lammermuir Hills on its long descent and banked steeply to the left to follow the Firth of Forth to make its final approach into Edinburgh airport. It was a journey Steven had often made in the past and he'd always enjoyed the moment when the two mighty bridges spanning the Forth came into view, but today he had too many other things on his mind to offer more than a grunt when the man in the seat beside him pointed out that all the scaffolding and sheeting had been removed from the Victorian rail bridge for the first time in years. 'They've finished painting it,' he said. 'New kind of paint; should last twenty-five years.'

Steven could only think that Jenny would be thirty-five years old when they painted the bridge again. She'd probably be married, probably have children – his grandchildren. He was wondering if she'd invite him for Christmas dinner when that image was interrupted by another, that of a group of mourners standing around a small white coffin. The hollow feeling in his stomach grew by the minute. The bump of the landing wheels didn't help.

His fellow passengers stood in readiness for the aircraft doors to open, an impatient file all looking remarkably the same in his eyes, about to spend their day maintaining their role in the great scheme of things, negotiating contracts, securing orders, jockeying for position on the career ladder, but at the end of the day it was odds on they'd all be going home to their families . . .

Steven turned his phone on as he made his way to the arrivals hall, walking past the row of name cards being held up along the route. He'd never had to pay these any attention before but today he did, simply because his actions were now to be determined entirely by somebody else. There was a Clarkson, written in green marker pen on cardboard, *Fenton – North Sea Gas* presented as a smudged computer print-out, even a rather grand card bearing the name Sir Peter Cross being held up by a man in chauffeur's uniform, but no Dunbar.

With no real sense of purpose or direction to guide him, Steven imagined he was getting an inkling of what it must be like to be excluded from society; an unpleasant feeling but another human cameo to add to his collection. He restored purpose by gravitating towards the nearest café and buying coffee, the assistant's inquisition about size and type irritating him more than usual. He sat down, placed his mobile on the table and waited for it to ring. It didn't.

At fifteen minutes past twelve Steven bought more coffee but didn't drink it. He needed neither the caffeine nor the attention of the woman whose task it was to clear away empty cups and sponge the table top with a cloth that smelt bad. At half past the hour his mind was going into overdrive, imagining all the awful things that could have happened, when he saw Ranjit Khan walking towards him. He was dressed in a smart suit that had not come off the peg and carried a laptop slung over his right shoulder. He was clean-shaven and his black hair was cut and styled to perfection. He looked every inch the successful lawyer or business executive. He smiled as he sat down beside Steven, shrugging his laptop strap off his shoulder to place the computer on the floor between them. It was a gesture Steven found slightly strange.

'Good morning, doctor. I apologise for my lateness. I've been watching you for the past forty minutes. You appear to be alone and you've just come off a flight so I know you're not armed: you wouldn't have risked it and there wasn't time to sort out permission. I take it you've brought what I asked for?'

'Where's my daughter, Khan?'

'All in good time,' replied Khan with the smug smile of a man who knew he was in charge.

'You're getting nothing until I see my daughter,' said Steven, his hands gripping the table edge as he struggled to keep them off Khan.

The smile faded from Khan's face. He placed his left hand on the table; it was clenched and holding something. Steven now understood why he hadn't used that hand to free the laptop strap.

'We don't have any time to waste. I have a flight to catch. Your daughter is in a car in the car park. When you turn on my laptop and put in the memory card to demonstrate decryption of the disk that's already in there, I will give you this.'

Khan raised his left hand but kept it clenched. 'This is a transmitter. As long as I keep the contacts open by maintaining pressure on a spring, nothing will happen. Should I let go . . . for any reason . . .' Khan watched to see that Steven had got the message, 'the circuit will complete and the car your daughter is currently locked inside will explode. If the card is genuine, I will transfer the transmitter to you very carefully and you can keep the contacts open until your daughter is found and freed . . . or until,' Khan glanced at the clock, 'twenty-three minutes have passed. After that, the car will explode anyway.'

197

'What car park is she in?' demanded Steven. 'This is an airport. There are lots of car parks, damn it.'

'One of them.'

'You bast—'

'Time is passing. I suggest you turn on the computer.'

Steven opened the case and slid out a Sony Vaio laptop. He pressed the On button, finding it hard to take his eyes away from Khan's clenched left fist as the machine powered up.

As the Windows jingle heralded the start of the session, Steven caught sight of Nick moving in the background. He sensed that the SAS man was looking for an angle that might give him the opportunity to shoot Khan without risk of hitting anyone else. This only added to Steven's rising sense of panic as he neared the moment when he must insert the fake card. Nick couldn't know about the triggering device in Khan's hand. He wanted to make eye contact and shake his head but recognised that that could be equally fatal, causing Khan to release the trigger arm of the device and start shooting his way out in the aftermath of an explosion which would cause widespread panic. The fact that the café was busy, however, was working in his favour. Nick couldn't risk it. He brought out the card from his inside pocket. 'How do we do this?' he asked.

'Start the disk then insert the card.'

Steven highlighted the disk drive and opened it to display gobbledegook on the screen.

'Now the card.'

All the anxiety of the past hours, the fear for Jenny's life, the regrets, the self-criticism, disappeared in an instant to be replaced by cold, calm resolve. The ability to act under extreme pressure had kicked in, the quality that Macmillan had seen in him a long time ago, the very reason he worked for Sci-Med. It was now or never.

Steven pretended to have difficulty looking for the memory card slot in a machine strange to him. He examined both sides of the laptop with exaggerated head movements, the second of these involving moving his elbow to deliberately knock over the full mug of coffee that was sitting on the table untouched. It flooded the keyboard, causing an immediate short circuit and blacking out of the screen.

In the tiny space of time that Steven anticipated he would have between shock registering on Khan's face and his taking any action, he threw himself at the former intelligence officer, having eyes for nothing but his left hand. He closed both his own hands round it and held it shut. He was now hopelessly vulnerable, unable to stop Khan using his right hand to probe for his eyes. He was relying on Nick to put a stop to that.

Nick duly obliged. He arrived beside the two struggling men on the floor as if trying to break up a fight but making sure he had his back to those in the café when he brought out his silenced pistol and ended Khan's life with a solitary body shot, which Steven noticed he even covered the sound of with a cough.

THIRTY-ONE

Breathlessly, Steven explained to Nick why he couldn't let go of Khan's hand until he had control of the triggering device. He told him quickly about Jenny and the unknown car park and Nick used his radio to call in the others in his group. At that moment the airport police arrived on the scene – two burly officers carrying sub-machine guns.

'Shut up and listen,' snapped Steven they launched into their routine. 'You'll find my ID in my pocket when I stand up. I'm a Sci-Med investigator on a code red. Verify this with your superiors then get chummy here to somewhere a bit more private. He's dead but let's pretend he isn't for the benefit of onlookers.'

He hoped that the people in the café wouldn't be too sure what to make of the scene they'd just witnessed. With any luck they might conclude it was an unseemly squabble over coffee spilt over a laptop with a third man wading in to break up the resulting melee. The police were now on the scene; order would soon be restored. No need to panic, no need to get involved.

Steven succeeded in transferring the trigger device from the dead man's hand to his own without releasing the spring. 'I need some tape,' he said to Nick as he got to his feet.

One of the police officers extracted Steven's ID and held his lapel radio to the corner of his mouth to relay details while the other looked on suspiciously, his finger loosely curled round the trigger of his weapon. He turned to Nick who had just returned with a roll of tape from one of the flight desks. 'And you are?'

'I'm with him.'

Steven held down the lever of the device while Nick taped it tightly so that it couldn't release.

'Yes sir, understood sir,' said the first policeman into his radio before returning Steven's ID and saying, 'Apparently we've to do whatever you say, doctor, until the brass arrive.'

'Close the airport to all traffic,' Steven said. 'All car parks have to be cleared of people and remain closed. There isn't time to clear the terminal buildings so keep people inside. One of the cars in one of the car parks is going to explode in . . .' Steven looked at the time. 'Eleven minutes.'

'Jesus,' said the policeman.

'There's a little girl trapped inside the car. I need . . . volunteer officers to help look for her. If they should come across her, they should report back before they touch anything. She may be wired . . . She's my daughter.'

'Christ almighty . . .'

'Get to it.' Steven turned to Nick, 'My impulse is to start running round the car parks at a hundred miles an hour like a headless chicken but we haven't a hope in hell of covering them all . . . so it has to be best guess time.'

'I don't see him using any of the outlying ones,' said Nick.

'Agreed,' said Steven. 'And I'm going to guess he's been using a hire car, probably from one of the big boys like Avis or Hertz, so that'll cut out a few makes and models. We can forget Range Rovers, sports cars and top-end marques. We're looking for an anonymous run-of-the-mill model in . . . I think he'd go for the nearest car park to the terminal: he had no reason not to. That means the multi-storey across the road. 'Agreed?'

Nick nodded. 'I'll get my guys to start from the top – one floor each. You and I can start from the ground up. How are we doing for time?'

'Nine minutes.'

Steven and Nick ran from the terminal building just as police vans, cars and fire appliances arrived. 'Maybe you could liaise with the police and bring them up to speed?' said Steven. 'I've got to look for her myself.'

'Sure,' said Nick with an understanding nod. 'Good luck.'

Steven started running round the deserted ground floor of the multi-storey, the fact that he was now alone allowing a tide of despair to encroach on him. Nick's final good luck wish now seemed to carry the same inflection it would have had he announced that he was going to jump over the moon. 'C'mon, c'mon,' he murmured. 'Give me a break . . . just one lousy break . . .'

He had just about completed his circuit of the ground floor when he heard shouting coming from somewhere above him. He stopped running and strained to hear what was being said, but at that moment a police loudhailer started warning personnel to withdraw from the area surrounding the car parks and drowned everything else out. It was a five-minute warning. An explosion was imminent: police on duty outside the car parks were being ordered to withdraw. Jenny had five minutes to live. Steven's anguish was interrupted when Nick called to reveal what the shouting had been about. 'She's on level three in a blue Ford Focus.'

Steven sprinted up the winding ramps like a man possessed. There was no need to look for the car: the three SAS men were already there. One was looking under the vehicle, the other two were examining the seams round the doors. One of them gestured to the back of the car and Steven looked in the rear window to see Jenny lying on the floor. Her eyes were closed and she wasn't moving. The fact that she wasn't gagged and didn't appear restrained in any way flagged up the nightmare that she was already dead. This threatened to overwhelm any sense of caution in him, especially when he noticed two electric wires wrapped round her ankle.

One of the SAS men had to stop him pulling the door open. 'Leave it to Stratocaster, mate. He knows what he's doing.'

Steven stepped back, to be joined by Nick who had now arrived on the scene.

'Well done, guys. How are we doing . . . with three minutes to go?'

'Door's okay,' said the soldier nicknamed Stratocaster, 'but I'd stand over there if I were you.'

Nobody moved. Stratocaster opened the rear door of the Ford slowly, feeling gingerly with his right hand round all the edges. 'So far so good . . .' He opened the door fully and, getting down on his hands and knees, started examining the floor of the interior with the aid of a torch. 'Here we go . . .' He had discovered the explosive device lodged under the front passenger seat. 'Another offering from IED Central . . .'

'There are a couple of wires round Jenny's ankle,' said Steven.

'Got them,' replied the soldier calmly.

Of course he'd bloody seen them, Steven admonished himself; he wasn't helping matters. He should move back but couldn't take his eyes off Jenny's lifeless face.

Stratocaster got on with the job, keeping up a running commentary as he went. 'Oh, I see . . . clever bastard . . . nearly had me there . . . let's see, blue for a boy connects to . . . nope, I tell a lie . . . it doesn't! It goes to the fu— Oh, very nice. Some bugger's been to the Afghan Academy for very naughty boys . . .'

The others exchanged nervous smiles as they listened to the muttering coming from inside the car until a snipping sound was followed by two others in quick succession and Stratocaster turned over on to his back to slide half out of the car and look up at them with a big smile on his face. 'Bang,' he said.

'Oh, you beauty,' exclaimed Nick as the tension evaporated from everyone bar Steven who was now anxiously bending over Jenny in the rear of the car. He touched her cheek and found it warm, causing him to give silent thanks.

'How is she?' asked Nick behind him.

'I think . . . she's going to be okay,' said Steven, struggling to get the words out against the wave of relief that flooded through him as he found the strong pulse in Jenny's neck. 'Fingers crossed she's just been kept sedated, but I'll have to get her to the sickbay in the terminal to check her out properly . . . but her pulse is strong and there's no sign of injury.'

'Great,' said Nick. 'Do you think we can tell the police the excitement's over?'

'Yep,' said Steven, allowing himself to relax with a heartfelt sigh. 'All over.'

'Good. Time for us to melt away then, before questions start being asked,' said Nick. 'We'll take all traces of the bomb with us, but I hope your people can deal with the clean-up across the road?'

Steven nodded. 'Of course.' He laid Jenny gently along the back seat in the car and shook the hand of each man in turn. 'I'm not sure I have the words to tell you what I feel right now,' he said. 'But I think you can guess. Thank you will have to do.'

'You would have done the same,' said Nick. 'That's the way we do things. We look after our own.'

Steven nodded, his throat tight. 'Damn right.'

Steven moved Jenny to the airport sickbay where he and the nurse were happy to conclude that she was just sleeping under the sedation Khan had given her. He called Tally's mobile to give her the news and heard her almost explode with joy before apparently turning away to speak to someone else.

This puzzled Steven. 'Where are you?' he asked.

'In Glenvane. I flew up to Glasgow this morning after your call and got the bus down. I'm with Peter and Sue and the kids. I thought we should all go through this together. God, what a relief. And Khan?'

'Gone from our lives.'

'Good. Sue's asking when we'll see you?'

'I'll wait here until Jenny comes round and then decide whether she needs a hospital check or not. If not – and I don't think she will – I'll bring her straight home.'

'I take it there was no official police involvement . . . I mean, no formal kidnap report filed?'

'No, there wasn't time. In the end it was down to just me and a few very . . . *very* good friends.'

'Must make the paperwork easier,' Tally joked uncertainly, as if dealing with conflicting emotions.

'Love you, Tally. See you later.'

'That has a nice ring to it.'

With Jenny still sleeping, Steven contacted Macmillan and told him all that had happened, apologising for not having kept him in the loop with time being so tight.

In the circumstances, Macmillan was understanding. 'Anything I can do to help?'

Steven told him that he had agreed with the soldiers that Sci-Med would make the necessary arrangements to remove Khan's body from the airport as their operation had been unofficial. Macmillan assured him that he would take care of it and also seek the Home Secretary's assistance in smoothing things over with Lothian and Borders Police, offering them Sci-Med's sincere thanks for their help and professionalism. The airport bomb incident could be dismissed as a false alarm.

'That should cover it,' agreed Steven. 'I'm going to hire a car to take Jenny home. I'll stay the night in Glenvane and be back in London tomorrow.'

'Did you get the disk?' asked Macmillan.

'Affirmative.'

'Good. I think the computer people have just about done everything they can so we should have a meeting as soon as possible to see if we can unravel just what the hell this has all been about.'

Jenny regained consciousness some thirty minutes later, giving a big yawn which made the airport nurse smile and Steven feel like a million dollars. 'Daddy, what are you doing here?' she asked, followed by a sleepy, 'Where am I?'

'You've been having rather a long snooze, nutkin,' said Steven, 'and you're in Edinburgh Airport, although we're not going anywhere. What do you remember, pussy cat?'

'A man . . . there was a bad man . . . he came to the house and hurt Uncle Richard . . . we were frightened . . . and . . . and then . . . nothing. I can't remember anything, Daddy.'

'He tried to steal you away, nutkin, but we wouldn't let him. He's gone now and he's never coming back,' said Steven, giving her a big hug. He was overjoyed that Khan appeared to have kept Jenny sedated the whole time. Working alone, he must have seen that as the easy option. From Jenny's point of view, there was no terror for her to remember, except of course the trauma of the break-in at the house in Glenvane. But even there she'd been sedated through the doctoring of her hot milk. She wouldn't even remember being taken from the house. It was better than he could ever have hoped for. With any luck, the scars should be minimal.

'Gosh, I'm thirsty,' said Jenny.

'And hungry too, I bet,' said the nurse. 'And I think we can fix both.'

THIRTY-TWO

Steven took a call from Macmillan. Arrangements had been made for an unmarked vehicle to pick up Khan's body and take it to the city mortuary for the night. From there it would be taken to East Fortune aerodrome, a small airfield in East Lothian, used mainly for recreational flying but occasionally by the military for flights they would rather remained unobserved, where it would be picked up for return to London and disposal as befitted an enemy of the state.

'Are we going home in Tarty, Daddy?' asked Jenny hopefully. The Boxster had been so christened after a comment Sue had made when she'd first laid eyes on it – 'A bit tarty, isn't it?' The children had overheard and the name had stuck.

'No, she's in Birmingham, nutkin. I flew up from there this morning. I've hired a car from the airport people for us to go home in.'

'Pity. I like Tarty.'

'Me too,' said Steven, thinking how good it was to see his daughter behaving as if nothing had ever happened. 'I'll bring her up soon and we'll zip around in her. Promise.'

With all three children upstairs in bed, Sue, Richard, Tally and Steven sat in front of the fire quietly acknowledging the departure of almost unbearable anxiety from their lives. It had been such an emotional time for all of them that adrenalin was now in very short supply and no one felt inclined to do anything other than sit and enjoy the warmth – both physical and mental – not to mention the malt whisky that Richard had opened.

'I'm so glad Tally thought to come up and join us, Steven,' said Sue. 'She put us right about a few things.'

Richard nodded his agreement but Steven looked at her questioningly.

'I think it fair to say that Richard and I were pretty angry with you and your job and the fact that it had brought us so much gut-wrenching worry – a classic case of needing something or someone to blame in times of crisis. But Tally pointed out something that made us think again. You do a very special job and you're good at it. We have no right to ignore that and you have the right to expect support from the people around you not whingeing and whining. As some politician said recently, we're all in this together, only in our case it's true.'

'Thank you,' murmured Steven. 'Believe me, I was only too aware of what you must be thinking . . . Thank you so much.' He gave Tally a special look of affection before closing his eyes and resting his head on the back of the chair. The hell of the past twenty-four hours was finally over.

Steven and Tally left early next morning to drive to Glasgow Airport, where Steven returned the car to the hire company before arranging flights for himself to Birmingham and for Tally to East Midlands Airport. He'd hoped that she might go with him to London but it was not to be: she had to get back on duty at the hospital where her colleagues had been covering for her.

'Call you later,' said Steven as his flight was called first.

Tally gave him a hug and said, 'Whoever said parting was such sweet sorrow was talking rubbish. It isn't.'

Steven drove to his flat in Marlborough Court to change before going to the Home Office where he found John Macmillan in Jean's office discussing where they should have the final meeting with the computer experts, who'd reported that they had deciphered as much as they could. Both turned as Steven entered and welcomed him back with sympathy and concern.

'It must have been an absolute nightmare for all of you,' said Jean. 'How is Jenny?'

Steven assured her that she was fine, and had missed most of the trauma by being kept under sedation.

'A blessing,' said Jean.

'I was just asking Jean where we could have the meeting,' said Macmillan.

'Seminar room twelve is free all afternoon,' offered Jean.

'Book it,' said Macmillan. 'And get hold of Scott Jamieson; he should be there. I've already asked Lukas Neubauer to come in now that we have the disk, and I've lodged a formal request for the release of the memory card. Let's try for three o'clock.'

'Very well, Sir John. I'll let everyone know.'

Macmillan ushered Steven through into his office. 'So, how are you? The last couple of days must have been pretty awful.'

'A fair summation,' Steven agreed, 'but it's over now. We were all very lucky, and . . . yes thank you, sir, I really am all right.'

Macmillan smiled. 'Good, because there's something I have to ask you.' He was no longer smiling.

'What would that be?'

'Khan's death. Who killed him?'

Steven thought for a moment before saying, 'What you're really asking is did I kill him. Did I execute Ranjit Khan because he killed my friend? The answer is no, I did not, and I have no further comment to make on the subject of his death.'

'Fair enough,' said Macmillan. The suggestion of a smile had returned.

Steven declined an offer of lunch, not for any reason other than the fact that he wanted to be alone with his thoughts. He bought sandwiches and shared them with the ducks in the park as he wondered with more than a little trepidation what the rest of the day would bring. His determination to see justice done for his friend had led him deeper and deeper into an investigation that had set him at loggerheads with what felt like half the governments of the western world and put his own daughter's life in mortal danger. The question he now had to wrestle with was . . . had it been worth it? Had it been an unswerving search for truth and justice or just a single-minded display of obstinacy on his part?

'A toughie,' Steven murmured as he threw the last of the crusts to the ducks and got up to go.

'Change of plan,' announced Macmillan when he saw him. 'The meeting is cancelled.'

Steven's puzzlement showed. Jean Roberts was no help; she just averted her eyes when he looked at her.

'I had a private debriefing with our computer experts and I've been able to make sense of their findings. I've thanked them and informed them that their services are no longer required. I've also reminded them that they are subject to the Official Secrets Act and, in their own interests, I am removing them from our retained consultants list. I've also suggested that it might be wise to omit their association with Sci-Med from their CVs.'

'Sounds like you're expecting some sort of backlash,' said Steven.

'If there is, I'm just trying to make sure that I'm the one to take it. I'm the one nearest retirement. I've cancelled our little get-together this afternoon because I've called a bigger one. You may remember that we were summoned to the Foreign Office not long ago to meet the great and the good who warned us off probing into the deaths of Simone Ricard and Aline Lagarde?'

'I do.'

'I have requested that the same people come here tomorrow at ten o'clock to hear what I have to say.'

'All of them?' exclaimed Steven, remembering the high-powered attendance at the last meeting.

'All of them. I'd like you, Scott Jamieson and Lukas Neubauer to be present.'

'Of course.'

Macmillan disappeared into his office, leaving Steven to expel his breath in a low whistle. He turned to Jean and asked, 'How on earth did he manage to get them all to agree?'

Jean smiled and whispered, 'Between you and me, he said they could either come and hear what he had to say . . . or read it in the *Telegraph*.'

'Wow,' said Steven. 'Respect.'

THIRTY-THREE

'Ladies and gentlemen, you summoned Sci-Med to appear before you some time ago. The purpose of that meeting was to assure us that the death of Dr Simone Ricard of *Médecins Sans Frontières* had been an accident and that the murder of her colleague, Dr Aline Lagarde, had been connected to Dr Lagarde's involvement in drug trafficking. My colleague and Sci-Med's chief investigator, Dr Steven Dunbar, did not believe you and neither did I. We were right.'

Macmillan had to pause to allow a hubbub of protest to die down. He looked around calmly at the angry faces and expressions of outrage as if he were auditioning actors for an amateur dramatics production. 'I am going to read you a statement outlining what we have since discovered and I would be grateful if you would allow me to do so without interruption.

'Dr Daniel Hausman, an American research scientist with CIA credentials working at Fort Detrick in the USA, made a very significant discovery. He discovered that the condition known as ME, or Chronic Fatigue Syndrome if you prefer, was caused by a virus. Not by a new virus, but by one that has been under the noses of researchers for years and whose presence would be dismissed as normal. The virus was the attenuated strain of polio virus used in the sugar lump vaccine to protect people across the globe against the scourge of polio.

'Hausman showed that the virus, alive and present in all individuals who'd received the sugar lump vaccine and also in those who'd subsequently been infected by it, could mutate under certain conditions and in response to certain triggers to cause the illness known as ME.

'In the belief that this finding would cause widespread panic among the many who'd received the vaccine, a cloak of secrecy was drawn over the findings by the US and UK governments and several others until such time as a method of inactivating the virus could be devised. Dr Hausman was seconded to Dr Tom North's lab in London to work on this – Dr North was an acknowledged world expert on the polio virus – and we believe scientists at the top secret establishments of Fort Detrick and Porton Down have also been working on it.

'Finding a way to inactivate the attenuated polio virus was considered so urgent that the governments of the UK and the USA in collusion with certain elements of the Pakistani government, agreed that experiments to test possible inactivators be carried out directly on human beings, to wit the population living in remote areas of the Afghan/Pakistan border. Meanwhile, the fear that some other researchers might stumble across the real cause of ME and announce it to the world led to a somewhat ludicrous MI5 operation designed to harass researchers in the field and discourage others from joining them. One of their stunts led to the death of the eminent microbiologist Professor Maurice Langley.

'It was inevitable that research establishments like Fort Detrick and Porton Down would also be interested in what might *activate* the latent virus as well as inactivate it. If this process could be controlled, they would have a weapon which could be used to render enemies weak and defenceless without the need for killing and destruction. Dr Mark McAllister, working at Fort Detrick, was successful in designing both an activator and an inactivator for the virus. He was due to meet British and Pakistani colleagues in the Afghan border region to report his findings when fate took a hand in the form of Dr Ranjit Khan.

'Khan, believed by the UK and US to be working with them as a member of Pakistani intelligence, had been collaborating with the CIA in the setting up of fake aid teams in order to carry out experiments but had an agenda of his own. He knew that the USA would be unlikely to share McAllister's findings so he set up an ambush in the mountains to steal the information. Khan's true allegiance was to a Pakistani extremist faction dedicated to the overthrow of Indian interests in the long-running dispute over territory in the north. Dr McAllister died in the ambush and the disk containing the data, along with a memory card designed to decrypt the disk, was taken to a remote village and left for Khan to collect at a later date.

'Before he could do so, however, Dr Simone Ricard of *Médecins Sans Frontières* and her vaccination team came across the remote village by accident and were disturbed by the numbers of sick people they found there. They took blood samples for analysis and also removed a computer disk and memory card when they left, believing them to contain evidence of shoddy polio vaccination schedules on the village children. She wanted to speak about this at a scientific meeting in Prague but was denied by the organisers, who believed they were acting in the best interests of aid to the region by covering up the use of a fake vaccination team put in by the CIA to gather information about the whereabouts of Osama Bin Laden.

'Khan followed Dr Ricard to Prague, hoping to recover the disk and card, but by that time she no longer had them. Khan killed her to keep her quiet about his interest and later murdered her colleague, Dr Aline Lagarde, in Paris – a good woman and dedicated aid worker whose reputation you trashed with the aid of French intelligence in order to stop any further investigation into their deaths, although by that time – when you warned us off – you must have known that something was gravely wrong.

'Khan's hunt for the information brought him to London where he murdered three more people: Dr Tom North, Dr Dan Hausman and a young PhD student, Liam Kelly. He obtained the disk but not the card which would make sense of it; however, he did discover that Dr Ricard had posted it to her friend and my colleague, Dr Steven Dunbar. It was Dr Dunbar's conviction that Simone Ricard and Aline Lagarde had been murdered that led him and Sci-Med to uncover the whole story. Khan's final gambit was to kidnap Dr Dunbar's daughter in an attempt to make him hand over the card. Happily, he failed in this and paid with his life.

'I leave it to you, ladies and gentlemen, to decide how proud you should feel of your actions. I am reminded of an old adage that says two can keep a secret if one of them is dead.

'We at Sci-Med have no further comment to make, although we do request that the restoration of Dr Lagarde's reputation be carried out as a matter of some urgency. We currently hold both the McAllister disk and the memory card. We presume that the US intended to share all aspects of the data with the UK and will hand it over to the relevant UK authorities so that work on deactivation of the latent virus can proceed without interruption. Our evidence that MI5 were complicit in discouraging biological research on ME will remain in our hands for the time being. We at Sci-Med greatly value our independence from all tiers of government. Thank you for your attention. We will not be taking questions.'

'Just a moment, Macmillan,' demanded a loud voice. 'What do you intend doing with this information?'

Macmillan, who was gathering up his papers, did not bother to look up to see who had asked the question. 'Nothing,' he replied. 'Our files will not be made public . . . unless, of course, any of us should take our own life in the woods.'

Followed by Steven, Scott Jamieson and Lukas Neubauer, he left the meeting, leaving a stunned silence behind him.

'I'm glad you got your knighthood before you said all that,' said Steven in an attempt to lighten the atmosphere as they walked back to the Home Office.

Macmillan managed a smile. 'You're not usually so sanguine at the end of an investigation.'

'It's an odd situation,' said Steven. 'Everyone thinks they did the right thing; everyone thinks they were acting in the best public interest and yet so many people ended up losing their lives.'

'I suppose no one could have anticipated Khan's appearing on the scene,' said Scott Jamieson.

There was silent agreement, but Steven wondered out loud when the CIA first realised that Khan had gone rogue.

'Wasn't it their man Andrews who told you?' asked Macmillan.

'I was armed at the time; he wasn't,' said Steven.

'Surely you don't think the CIA were complicit in all these deaths?' said Scott Jamieson.

'No, I don't, but I think it may have suited their purpose not to let on to Khan that they knew who he was really working for until he'd tidied things up for them. I think Andrews let him see my file in the hope that he would remove the problem of Sci-Med's interest in what they'd been up to.'

After a few moments' silence, Macmillan said, 'The first one to say oh what a tangled web we weave pays for lunch.'

No one did.

'All right, I'll pay,' said Macmillan. 'Let's collect Jean first.'

Steven's mobile rang during the meal and he excused himself. It was Tally. 'How did it go?'

'John was brilliant. I'll tell you all about it later.'

'Then you're coming up tonight?'

'You bet.'

'It's something you won't have to do for much longer,' said Tally.

'You mean . . . ?' exclaimed Steven.

'Yep, I got the job.'

216

AUTHOR'S NOTE

Although *The Secret* is a work of fiction, the story was inspired by fact. The CIA did carry out a fake anti-polio vaccination programme in the Pakistan/Afghanistan border region in their efforts to hunt down Osama Bin Laden. This of course put many children at risk and damaged trust in genuine aid teams working in the area. At the time of writing, the region is still one of the few areas in the world where polio remains endemic.

In July 2011 the BBC reported a 'torrent of abuse' hindering ME/Chronic Fatigue Syndrome research. They reported harassment of scientists working on the problem including death threats, vilification on internet websites and complaints alleging personal and professional misconduct made to authorities including the General Medical Council.

The BBC quoted Professor Simon Wessely of King's College London saying, 'It's direct intimidation in the sense of letters, emails, occasional phone calls and threats.' Professor Wessely went on to say, 'Sadly, some of the motivation seems to come from people who believe that any connection with psychiatry is tantamount to saying there is nothing wrong with you, go away, you're not really ill.'

The ME Association's Dr Charles Shepherd condemned the abuse of researchers but said sufferers had a justifiable complaint that almost no government-funded research was looking at the bio-medical aspects of the illness.

Professor Myra McClure of Imperial College London, who was subjected to abuse after virologists failed to replicate findings of

217

a reported link to the XMRV retrovirus, was quoted as saying, 'It really was quite staggeringly shocking, and this was from patients who seemed to think I had some vested interest in not finding this virus. I couldn't understand, and still can't to this day, what the logic of that was. Any virologist wants to find a new virus.'

Professor McClure decided not to continue research on the subject.